Praise for Jane Mendelsohn's

AMERICAN MUSIC

"How can something so slim cover so much ground? This breadth is achieved through a series of haunting impressions that trace the story of a family, the history of twentieth-century America, and the evolution of American music. . . . It is a testament to Mendelsohn's skill that she can decode a lifetime in an image."
— *The New York Times Book Review*

"Luminous. . . . Intricately plotted and affectingly written. . . . A piercing, magical revelation about the capricious power of disclosed truths to lift us up or take us down."
— *The Boston Globe*

"Jane Mendelsohn captures [details] as you might in the glare of an old-fashioned flashbulb; a reader is left blinking, uncertain of what she has imagined."
— *Los Angeles Times*

"Romantic and lush. . . . A novel about the power of stories. . . . [Mendelsohn] writes the kind of lovely, wise phrases that will have you underlining passages. . . . [A] sophisticated novelist who can still cast that primal enchantment."
— *The Washington Post*

"If the artist Edward Hopper had been a writer, he might have dreamed up something like the New York–y 1930s sections of Jane Mendelsohn's *American Music*, a beautiful, bittersweet novel."
— *O, The Oprah Magazine*

"Intriguing. . . . Haunting. . . . Dips boldly into the waters of magical realism. . . . Even though life often plays in a minor key, it can be perfect sometimes anyway."
—*The Miami Herald*

"In her exquisite, psychologically fluent novels, the actual and imagined merge as Mendelsohn tests the power of stories to define, guide, and sometimes destroy us. Her third novel is an intricate puzzle of haunting, far-reaching, secretly connected love stories. . . . Sensuously rendered." —*Booklist* (starred review)

"Beautifully rendered. . . . [Joe, Pearl, and Vivian's] story is a heartbreaker, stark in its reality. . . . Powerful. . . . Hard to forget." —*The Providence Journal*

"Invites the kind of reading we don't often allow ourselves anymore—that accomplished in one sitting. . . . Mendelsohn allows each of these stories to arrive at what feels like its natural end, like cymbals allowed to tremble until they gradually come to rest." —*Slate*

"As in her earlier novel, *I Was Amelia Earhart*, Jane Mendelsohn proves a master of historical context: American history itself is as much a character as those who live and die through it."
—*The Post & Courier* (Charleston)

"Jane Mendelsohn has produced a taut, sui generis story that should be a major contender for novel of the year. . . . Brilliant, stunning and divinely thought-provoking." —*Sacramento Book Review*

"Haunting, mystical and beautiful, *American Music* is written in a uniquely creative style that poignantly and powerfully touches the reader contemplating the gift of music in an American period of history yearning for recovery and renewal." —*Historical Novels Review*

"Mendelsohn has created characters who are so deeply sympathetic, so believably flawed and interesting. . . . Suspenseful and compelling. . . . The revelatory conclusion is richly satisfying. . . . An inventive, passionate, pithy novel whose major theme is love itself and whose minor theme, music, is an emotional, meaningful counterpoint." —*Elle*

Jane Mendelsohn

AMERICAN MUSIC

Jane Mendelsohn is a graduate of Yale
University. She is the author of two previ-
ous novels, including the *New York Times*
bestseller *I Was Amelia Earhart.* She lives in
New York City with her husband and two
children.

www.janemendelsohn.com

ALSO BY JANE MENDELSOHN

I Was Amelia Earhart

Innocence

AMERICAN MUSIC

JANE MENDELSOHN

AMERICAN MUSIC

Albany County
Public Library
Laramie, Wyoming

Vintage Contemporaries
Vintage Books
A Division of Random House, Inc.
New York

FIRST VINTAGE CONTEMPORARIES EDITION, JUNE 2011

Copyright © 2010 by Jane Mendelsohn

All rights reserved. Published in the United States by Vintage Books, a division of
Random House, Inc., New York, and in Canada by Random House of Canada
Limited, Toronto. Originally published in hardcover in the United States by
Alfred A. Knopf, a division of Random House, Inc., New York, in 2010.

Vintage is a registered trademark and Vintage Contemporaries and colophon are
trademarks of Random House, Inc.

This is a work of fiction. Names, characters, places, and incidents either are the
product of the author's imagination or are used fictitiously. Any resemblance to
actual persons, living or dead, events, or locales is entirely coincidental.

Grateful acknowledgment is made to Nick Cave for permission to reprint an excerpt
from "The Ship Song" by Nick Cave. Reprinted by permission of Mute Song Ltd.
on behalf of Nick Cave.

The Library of Congress has cataloged the Knopf edition as follows:
Mendelsohn, Jane, 1965–
American music / by Jane Mendelsohn.—1st ed.
p. cm.
1. Families—Fiction. I. Title.
PS3563.E482A8 2010
813'.54—dc22 2009037382

Vintage ISBN: 978-0-307-47397-4

Book design by Iris Weinstein

www.vintagebooks.com

Printed in the United States of America
10 9 8 7 6 5 4 3 2 1

TO MY PARENTS,

TO MY DAUGHTERS,

AND, ALWAYS,

TO NICK

O boys, this story
The world may read in me: my body's mark'd
With Roman swords.

— WILLIAM SHAKESPEARE, *Cymbeline*

If you expect happy days, look out.

— BILLIE HOLIDAY, *Lady Sings the Blues*

PART ONE

CHAPTER ONE

2005

She stands up in the subway car where she has been sitting and looks out into the darkness. Her stop is coming and she likes the moment before the light breaks through the window. There is her reflection in the glass, a ghost with a shifting skeleton and a visible heartbeat as the columns and dim lights that make up the architecture of this underworld scroll through her body rapid-fire in the blackness. Then she disappears into the light. She turns toward the doors. She adjusts the strap of the bag slung across her chest and quickly steps onto the platform.

It is raining softly when she emerges onto the street. From a distance, she appears to be marching, silently, through the mist. With her steady gaze and long coat, her faded satchel and heavy boots, she looks both present and ancient. She looks like some beautiful soldier arrived from history.

She walks several blocks along empty gray streets toward a large white undistinguished building. In the lobby of the building she shows an identification card and rides up in the elevator. She steps off and walks down a hall. A door is open for her. Inside, a man is lying chest down on a table, a thin white sheet covering his body. His hand lifts slightly when she enters.

You're here, she says.

I'm here, he says.

That's something, she says.

It is.

Every week she pulls down the sheet and studies his back. She washes her hands and oils them and then rubs the oil onto the skin. His hands clench when she starts to work. He seems to be experiencing something more than pain. As she touches him there is transmitted to her bones his fierce desire to remain separate. He is determined not to reveal his secrets. She has visited him for weeks and she knows his back by now, the flat plane between the shoulder blades, the slope down to the sacrum. But she knows only his back, his neck, his arms, his legs. He will only lie on his front. He will never lie on his back, never let her work on his chest or face. He will not tell her why. She knows only that he has seen more than he can share, and she was told during the interview that she would have to respect his privacy. These men are suffering, the nurse had cautioned her. These men are haunted.

Still, there were stories in his body that she searched for like a detective. She had begun to feel as though she could read him, as if she could interpret the meaning in his knots and sinews. Sometimes, and this was not the first time she had questioned her sanity, she received visions from his limbs, his muscles, his bones. The first time it had happened she was touching his ankle when there arose in her mind the image of a woman standing underwater in a shaft of light, her dark hair wafting weightlessly like ink. Then her hand reached his neck and she saw more people. At first, they appeared to be moving to music, glittering couples swaying on a dance floor. But then in a shift of perspective she saw hundreds of bodies, each alone, swaying upright underwater. An underwater graveyard with thousands of unseeing eyes staring directly at her.

Suddenly, she felt sick. The light changed outside, the sky grew darker, and in the small dim room the body on the table seemed to break beneath her touch. Then from inside that, as if it were a hollowed-out broken sculpture, came pouring waves of water. She placed her hands on the man's back until she could not see the swaying bodies any longer. She took a breath. For the moment, there were no more visions. She was safe. Yet within him, she knew, were only more stories. For a soldier's body is a work of art that contains his country's history.

You were saying something in your sleep, she said.
No, he said.
Yes, you were trying to tell me something.
He whispered something inaudible, then nothing. She had her hand on his arm and in a sudden flash she saw a pair of cymbals made of burnished beaten metal. She thought she could hear the reverberations of their clanging, as if from a great distance. Then she looked down at

his face and saw the rapid uncontrollable movement of his eyelids. He was sleeping, but he was not at peace.

He began to speak again. This time it was clear and she could make out most of the words. He described an elaborate ballroom and dancing with his hand pressed firmly against a woman's back. He talked about someone who disappeared. "For years I looked for her in the jungle, in the desert. I saw her face on the body of a tiger." He opened his eyes but he was still sleeping. She looked into those eyes and they were shining, metallic. What was he trying to tell her?

We died that night at Roseland.

He said they fell in love because of the music. Count Basie was making his New York debut on Christmas Eve at the Roseland Ballroom. The Count and the reflections of the Count on the instruments swayed slightly when he lifted his arm. He turned in time to the beat and his image danced along the line of brass, so that although he was gracefully and confidently conducting his orchestra he appeared to be imprisoned inside the music. He took a seat at the piano. He nodded his head. The music swung. The bodies on the dance floor moved like thoughts in one consciousness, bubbles in a glass of champagne.

He said he put his hand on a woman's back. He pulled her close. When they danced they danced slow and that's when he knew that the music would kill them both.

On the dance floor there were hundreds of us, swaying upright like moving tombstones.

Is this a dream? she asked.

No, he said.

When did it happen?

1936.

1936

Joe lifted his black saxophone case with one hand and with the other he picked up his brown leather suitcase. He used his arm to push his hat a little bit back on his head. He watched the city coming toward him. Over the railing in the water the reflection of the skyline slid closer with its gray syringe buildings shooting straight ahead like a metal tray of instruments being handed to a doctor.

He would not have known what to do with them. He was a musician. The boat pulled in lazily to the harbor and the air tasted like salt and dirt and real silver. Across the green expanse of river he saw a milling crowd. In that instant he lived peacefully with the certain knowledge that he would be met with an embrace. His wife would be there. He couldn't help smiling.

Someone's happy to be home, a stranger said to him.

Welcome to New York City, Joe said.

The sun was strong although shrouded now and then by clouds and he was hot in his best suit. When the ship finally pulled in he saw the cumulus blow away to reveal a powder blue sky. The heat surged, causing the passengers on the deck to shift uncomfortably and then remove various items, gloves, scarves. Everyone was overdressed. By the time the liner docked most people were disheveled and in the excitement of arrival had overcome their usual propriety. Strangers spoke to strangers. Those who had become friends during the crossing bade farewell, exchanged addresses, shed tears. It was as if the assembled had gathered for a wedding or a funeral on this sunny morning in September. He closed his eyes and let a last gasp of ocean air hit his face.

The dock was shadowed by the great ship and crowded. A watery light filtered down from on high and seemed to float between the bodies. He moved with a steady grace through the throng. He passed a woman standing amidst twelve pieces of well-traveled luggage. She recognized him from her time at the captain's table, and as he walked by she grabbed hold of his arm to tell him how much she had enjoyed him, his playing. He had hardly time to thank her he was moving so quickly, searching the faces. A flash of anger pierced his thoughts when he considered that Pearl might not be there but then he reconsidered. He stepped beyond the center of the crowd into the brightness where he saw a man holding a birdcage. When the man bent down to get something the space behind him revealed a gray hat with a white feather. It was her best hat.

Pearl did not see him. She was looking just to the left of him, beyond him, and she was beautiful. She was beautiful in a simple, lovely way that he knew like he knew a song. Her eyes were squinting a little and she held a small piece of paper in her small hand and standing next to her and clearly with her was someone he didn't know, a woman. The woman was looking also at the crowd, or past it, and seemed to be saying something to Pearl. In all likelihood she was asking her what he looked like but the expression on the woman's face was so calm and unquestioning that she might have been talking about something completely unrelated. It was as though she was not aware of the movement around her, or if she was, it did not concern her. She seemed to occupy her own air. She was taller than Pearl. She was wearing sunglasses.

As he approached and Pearl saw him her lipsticked lips burst apart and she rushed toward him and held him and the person next to her stood still in her own atmosphere. Only after he and Pearl had kissed and he had stroked her temples and eyelids with his thumb and she had clasped her hand on the back of his neck and they had said hello with their eyes did the air open up around the other person enough for him to actually look at her face. That's when he observed the curve of her cheek, like a dangerous road, and the elegant line of her mouth. In each of the lenses of her round sunglasses floated a tiny, perfect ship.

Still, he could not quite look at her.

2005

The hospital was the oldest veterans' hospital in New York. It stood atop a hill on the highest point in the city, a spot that had been a strategic vantage point during the Revolutionary War. In 1847 the millionaire William Bailey, later of Barnum & Bailey Circus, had built an estate on this location for his bride. In 1922 the veterans' bureau had bought the land and set up a hospital for veterans suffering from mental and nervous disorders. In 1970 *Life* magazine had run a feature on the hospital exposing its deplorable conditions. Paralyzed vets lay on one side for ten hours without being moved or washed. Without enough attendants to empty them, the urine bags to which the men were hooked up spilled over onto the floor. When and if they were given a shower, the men could wait helplessly for hours to be dried, and often they were put back into bed on the same sweaty sheets. There were rats. A paralyzed veteran might suddenly awaken to find a rat on his hand. He could not move his hand, so he would try to jerk his shoulders. He screamed, and the rat jumped casually off the bed. In the paraplegic ward, a completely crippled patient would depend on a buddy who still had the use of his arms to get a sheet thrown, sailing and rippling and falling like a shroud, over his bed.

As a result of the *Life* magazine exposé, the hospital was overhauled and conditions were vastly improved. More than thirty years later those who were aware enough of their circumstances to appreciate them, or the families of those who weren't, felt lucky to be living or have their loved ones living in this hospital and not in a bad hospital and not out on the streets. The ever-increasing number of homeless veterans was a decades-old national tragedy. During the day they lingered in the parks and on the sidewalks. They sat beside signs scrawled on cardboard boxes in which had been shipped computers and flat-screen televisions and imported foods and kitchen appliances. The faces of the soldiers looked stricken and lined and their eyes blinked in the rays of sunlight that beat down on them like the unstoppable force in civilian life of their own private wars.

The woman was also happy to be working in the hospital and not to be out on the streets. She was nearly alone in this world. Her name was Honor. Her soldier's name was Milo.

·

Is that too much? she asked.

No, he said.

She warmed more oil in her hands and rubbed her way down his arm. She loved the strong wrists, the length of his fingers, each bone like the neck of a small animal, the hollow of his palm. Reaching the center of his hand she pressed gently, then with more force, and he winced, breaking her trance.

That spot, he said. You told me once before what it was called.

In the center of your palm?

Yes.

In Chinese medicine?

Yes.

The Palace of Anxiety.

He made a sound that was almost a laugh.

1936

The three of them stood in the September heat still and formal like too many figures on a wedding cake. Then Pearl took Joe's hand and squeezed it and looked up at him saying weren't they lucky it wasn't raining it was supposed to rain and then said oh and the most marvelous thing my cousin Vivian is in town. Here she is. I don't think the two of you have ever met, have you?

Joe was sweating quite a bit now. He wiped his hand flat

on his white shirt and held it out to the woman with the ships in her eyes.

No, I don't think so, he said.

She did not lean forward to reach his hand. She held out hers and he took it. Hello Vivian, he said. Still, he felt he could not really see her face.

You must be Joe. She had a quiet voice that seemed to emerge from someplace outside of her, from her dark hair, her patterned scarf. It's nice to meet you Joe. It was a voice that had a slight tremble in it, like the beating of a bird's wing.

He picked up his saxophone case and his suitcase in one gesture with Pearl still holding on to his arm. The woman seemed very comfortable with silence. It made him nervous. Were you waiting long? They said the ship would be on time but we took forever to pull in . . . The round sunglasses reflected cars now as they walked toward the street.

Pearl grabbed his arm with both of hers. I would have waited for you all day, she said.

Only a day? he said.

A day and a half. She smiled.

The woman walked a little ahead of them, politely, although it didn't entirely feel polite. She took off her scarf and tied it loosely around the strap of her handbag.

The car is up the block, Pearl said, hurrying beside him to keep up with his long stride.

Vivian walked on ahead and the scarf slid off from her handbag and fell to the ground. Joe pulled away from Pearl instinctively and ran up a ways and bent down to the sidewalk and he picked up the scarf with his hand still holding his saxophone case. She was standing by the car.

You dropped this, he said.

Oh thank you, she said. That was careless of me.

She took the scarf.

Pearl walked slowly toward them in the heat.

I hope I didn't spoil your homecoming, Vivian said. Pearl insisted that I join her.

It's nice to have a welcoming committee, he said.

Not always, she said.

She was looking right at him. He could not see through her glasses.

Yes it is, he said. Always.

They drove uptown. The air blew in the windows hot as smoke. They drove up the West Side Highway, alongside the Hudson River which shimmered white in the heat, past ferry and ship terminals and some warehouses and then out into the open where they could see New Jersey across the water green like the countryside. They passed low buildings on their right, seedy hotels and bars for sailors, cheap restaurants with a chair and table out front. Then Joe said he was sick of the water and missed the city so they turned off the highway and headed across midtown where the buildings shadowed their little vehicle like the bodies of prehistoric beasts. Up Eighth Avenue the stores were to the trade only and then he sped up Sixth where the people's clothes got fancier and the store signs were written in elegant cursive or clean bold print. Joe drove and Pearl sat next to him and Vivian sat in the back-seat with her profile cutting into the rearview mirror, a precise cameo. She answered his questions about how she was related to Pearl, on her mother's side, where she'd grown up, in Brooklyn, where she'd been lately, to Europe. She had gone to college, on scholarship, which explained a little bit about her demeanor, so different from Pearl's.

She'd been studying art, in Italy, on a fellowship, until recently, when she'd come back. Her father was sick. For now she was living at home.

Then he realized that she barely knew Pearl. Pearl had grown up on the West Coast and had never been east until she'd met and married Joe. Vivian must have been encouraged by her parents to call Pearl. He had a vague memory of his wife mentioning family in Brooklyn, maybe they'd even visited once.

So you're the East Coast branch of Pearl's family, he said. The intellectuals.

And you're the musician.

The law student. He looked at Pearl.

Yes, Pearl told me, she said. It's nice that your music can pay for school. How often do you do that, play on ships?

A few times a year. I know a band or two that will take me when they go overseas. The money is good. But I get homesick. He reached over and took Pearl's hand.

Of course, Vivian said.

They were driving up Central Park West now, along the park. The trees swayed and rustled like enormous skirts.

Vivian dances, Pearl said.

Not really, Vivian said. Not anymore.

Well you used to. Your mother told me that you were a wonderful dancer. She said you went to all kinds of places, jazz places, way uptown, the Savoy.

Really? Joe said.

I like that kind of music, she said quietly, still looking out the window.

So does Joe, Pearl said. He plays it beautifully.

Does he, Vivian said.

In the rearview mirror he could see the park receding, the green light of the trees, their colors, pulling away.

We should all go hear some music together, he said. Hear some music and dance.

Milo

He sat in his wheelchair in his room staring out the window. He always did that after she left. His thoughts spun around in his head, images that she had unleashed just by touching him, a string of memories, some of which were his own but most of which were not, could not be, from his life. He thought he was finally going crazy. He was surprised it had taken this long. He watched visions stream past like the radically changing scenery out the window of a swift train. He saw the green trees pulling away from him in the mirror of an old car and a profile cut like a cameo. A voice asked him when he had started to play music and he could not remember that he had ever picked up an instrument. Maybe in elementary school he had been taught the recorder, or in high school plucked a guitar for a few months. He could see that ahead of him a streetlight was changing from red to green and the sun was slicing between the buildings on his left side, where there appeared to be a river, just out of sight. He was heading up a wide street and saw the store signs jauntily bouncing past, vendors on the sidewalks, rounded cars like giant toys rolling beside him and parked at the curb but he could not remember having driven in such a city and all the places he had driven were now jumbled together in a crazy highway of his past. The street he'd grown up on, leafy and almost always empty, turned into the rolling road to Blue Hill where he'd gone to high school which became a cobbled street in Germany which merged into the dusty desert under the convoy, his mother driving him home . . .

Everything flew by, a freeway of memories that were his but then as quickly as they ribboned past they would change into places such as this broad city street of another era and he was saying, as clearly as he had ever said anything, that he had first picked up a trumpet when he was five. He had done no such thing. But he was saying it, saying it with the warm wind on his neck, saying it to a woman in a backseat. He had witnessed this, no, inhabited it, while lying on the table in the little room. And now it would not leave his mind.

Next he was heading past the park entirely, up a hill where the apartment houses gave way to brownstones lining the streets like gentle dogs sitting side by side and beside him in the passenger seat a woman, evidently his wife, was singing softly but he couldn't hear the song. He was making some kind of progress toward a destination, but in this unfamiliar memory everything seemed slowed down, moving through water. It was as though the woman next to him singing, the warm wind, the profile in the rearview mirror, the houses rolling by, the wide sky turning gently silver-gray, it was as though it was all happening in real life while he himself sitting in this hospital room was only a dream, imagined by a man driving a car through Harlem on a September afternoon.

He stared out the window and it was not September. It was some other month, some other world. The room was dark now, and the lights were turning on in the hallways and soon he would not be able to see anything but his reflection. He did not look forward to that. His face was a mess. His face was a reminder. Not of ships docking or of dancing at the Savoy but of dust and sun and fire. There were no fires left in him, he thought, only the memory of fire. This was his life now: cold and unlit and lived in a small room. All that remained after the fire had burned out was this ineffective body, this savaged face. But then he remembered the stories she stirred up in him and for a moment he sensed a living heat like an ember in his chest.

He wheeled away from the window. He could not get into his bed without assistance so he sat there looking at it. It had been his bed for a while now and he had developed a fierce attachment to it that he recognized was both understandable and absurd. He had slept in many beds over the years but this was the only one for which he had ever felt an affection. It was not a nice bed. The white sheets smelled sour from detergent and the thin pillow looked up at him forlornly but he took comfort in its simplicity. He needed it. He had no stillness inside.

For example he could feel a kind of music playing quietly, endlessly, inside of him. It was the shimmering sound of cymbals. He could barely hear it but whenever he strained to listen it would fade away almost completely and only return when he wasn't paying attention. He tried to ignore it, to trick it into turning up the volume. He used to play music in his room so loud, he remembered, stupid

teenage radio music that seemed idiotic and very beautiful
to him now, so loud that the windows shook.

Eventually a nurse came in and helped him into bed. He
heard the distant reverberation of cymbals. He saw his
bedroom from childhood, the window which looked out
at the tree, his shelf of trophies with their figures suspended in action, his clothes pooled on the floor. The cymbals continued, glistening beneath his thoughts. Then he
saw what he had seen just this morning with her, the wide
thoroughfare, the patterned scarf, a ship. He closed his
eyes and remembered what had come to him like a memory but which was not his and yet by now had truly
become a part of him. He was stunned by the vividness of
the sensation of driving a car and feeling the wind. He
knew what it was like to lose sensation and so he appreciated and savored these feelings. That this sensitivity was
all in his mind was something for which he felt deeply
grateful, an astonishing accomplishment of the human
brain, and for a moment it seemed as if it was all that really
mattered. But then he thought about his legs and he
decided that real life actually mattered very much. He
remembered this and the pain in his mind was as piercing
and as deep as always.

1936

They drove farther uptown. They drove through Harlem,
where Vivian pointed out some of the places she knew,
then up to Inwood and into the Bronx. In University

Heights the apartment houses shaded the sidewalks and left the streets lurking in a blue haze at this hour. Joe suggested that they stop at one of their favorite neighborhood restaurants to celebrate his return but Pearl insisted that they go home because she'd already bought groceries for dinner. Vivian had left her bag in the apartment, having stayed over the night before, which was why she had come home with them. She said she would just run upstairs to get it and be gone. Joe and Pearl implored her to stay for dinner. She did not want to intrude. They must want some time alone, she said. She agreed to stay for a cup of coffee.

Upstairs she collected her belongings. She had stayed over because Pearl had heard from her aunt that there was no room in their house with Vivian's father sick and the nurse and so many visitors. Pearl had offered to have Vivian stay even longer. Vivian said it was wonderful to get to know each other a little after all these years but that she really wanted to be closer to Brooklyn to be able to help her family. In the kitchen Pearl was warming coffee on the stove and setting out some cookies on a plate. There was a small table in the kitchen and four chairs. From a little window facing the Hudson the setting sun sent a lavender and yellow cast over the table, the chairs, the plate of cookies. It was a soft yet acidic light. Joe sat down at the table and took a cookie. Pearl put a thick white cup filled with coffee in front of him. He took a sip. When he looked up Vivian was standing in the doorway.

She was not wearing her sunglasses. She had pinned up her hair. In the weird lavender light she looked like a luminous marble statue. Her eyes were a shade of green that he had never seen before. She stood still in the doorway as if on the threshold of an unknown body of water. She glanced at him for an instant with a questioning look, an expression that so far he had never seen on her face. It was as though she were asking him if it was okay to come in, should she brave the water, would she be safe? He held her gaze. A strand of dark hair fell in front of the outside corner of her eye and down her cheek. Suddenly he was not afraid of anything. He looked at her for what seemed like a long time and she came over and sat down at the table.

Sipping her coffee in the now more orange-tinted light she no longer had that look on her face. She seemed indifferent: to the humble apartment, the plain kitchen, the happy couple. She sat very calmly with her delicate fingers wrapped around the cup, her thin wrist sticking out of her sleeve. But Joe felt that he had been allowed to glimpse something private and that now he understood her a little bit. She was not so composed. A pleasurable weakness swept through him. It made him feel strong. He felt as though a secret had been revealed to him and he was certain that his life would go on this way, a series of revelations. He was beginning to understand things. He felt light and clear and in control of his destiny. He thought he was becoming a man. He did not think that the green eyes and the lavender light could account for such a feeling. That was not possible.

2005

At night she reads his bones. Honor watches them as they fly toward her in the darkness, spinning, burning, aflame. They arrange themselves into letters, then words. They spell out secrets that she doesn't want to know. As each word is extinguished, it leaves a pile of white ashes. The last word flickers, glowing, for a long time. It is Fate.

CHAPTER TWO

Milo

Some lives were pieced back together. Sometimes this happened in the hospital. There were veterans who played piano. There were those who watched movies. Some read books. Some told jokes. Not all of them told jokes. In the Bronx VA hospital some of those suffering from mental and nervous disorders told jokes incessantly, and some never spoke. Many of them had sustained major physical injuries as well as psychological illnesses. Milo Hatch had sustained a spinal cord injury. At the moment, he could not walk. The prognosis was not good. He exhibited symptoms of acute post-traumatic stress disorder. He had nightmares. He woke up screaming. During the day, he rarely spoke, and then only if it was a necessity. As time went by the doctors and nurses and other hospital staff members came to accept Milo's silence and he came to know his predictable environment well enough to get along without much language. Then one day as part of his physical therapy and rehabilitation he was introduced to a person who was going to be giving him what the nurse referred to as therapeutic bodywork. A young woman walked up to him and held out her hand. He looked at her hand and it appeared to burst into flames. He looked at the hand and it was again a hand. He pushed the button on his wheelchair and speeding past her he rolled out the door and down the corridor and back to his room. The young woman with her long hair and heavy boots stood looking out the open door. The nurse in her modest uniform stared at her. In these white scrubbed rooms and clean empty hallways the nurses did not like to see outside practitioners. The woman understood the territorial expression on the nurse's face and picked up her messenger bag and put on her long coat and said that she would try again next time.

A crisis came when the doctors told Milo that he would be required to submit to therapeutic bodywork. This meant that he would have to be alone with the woman with the fiery hands. Helplessly, he argued with the doctors. He used more words than he had since his arrival and, privately, his doctors were pleased by his sudden progress. He was escorted to the dim room with the drawn shades. A frantic desire to hide roamed his body. He didn't know how to escape. He could never find a position on the table that was comfortable. While he fled into his fantasies the woman, whose name was Honor, stood by his body with her bottles of oils and kneaded his resistant flesh. Her hair was long and wavy and when she worked she pulled it back into a loose bun. When she was working like this she sometimes sang quietly to herself in a voice that was slightly but pleasingly off-key. Her songs were just tunes with no lyrics that she remembered from some long-ago time and faraway place.

One afternoon she began to work on the man's hands for the first time. He kept them clenched into fists. She looked at them and asked him if he could unclench his fingers. He said nothing, but turned his head to one side in a gesture that seemed to indicate that he was trying to open them but he could not. She took a liberty and pried open the fingers of his left hand. He allowed it. When all five fingers were released she began to rub the center of his palm. There were no visions this time but a shattering pain rushed up her arm and stopped in the back of her eye. She pulled her hands off of his palm, shaking. With his right hand the same thing happened. She pulled her hands off again. She told him that they were done for the day. That was the beginning.

I can't go.

You'll feel better, said the nurse.

No I won't. His head was pounding this morning. He didn't want to see that woman. A scarf was lying at the foot of his bed.

What's that doing there? Milo said.

What? the nurse said.

That silk scarf.

Your T-shirt, she said, picking it up.

She put it away and helped him out of bed. She wheeled him down the corridor. Of course he could wheel himself but they wanted to make sure that he arrived at his destination. He had been known to pretend to go for his session, only to be found later in the lounge watching television. This seemed more important, he would say. The nurses had a difficult time resisting his charms even though he wasn't exactly charming. The one with the smile, they called him. He had a lopsided chipped-tooth unafraid smile. He used it sparingly. Usually he just grinned with his lips closed but it was a welcoming, dangerous grin. He was suffering, no one could forget that, and he was not immune to wanting others to suffer with him.

The harsh fluorescent lights were on in the little room. She was waiting for him. She stood with her back to the door and she was putting up her hair. When she turned around she had bobby pins in her mouth and with them still in her mouth she said, Hey. Her voice, her face, her eyes, her mouth, there was no danger in any of it. So why was he so afraid of her?

I thought you weren't coming, she said. Like last week.

Sorry about that.

The nurse helped him onto the table. His upper body was very strong now, and Honor noticed for the first time the way he pulled himself up with his big arms.

He thinks he can get away with anything, the nurse said. Then she left the room.

Honor turned down the lights. I thought we'd try something different, she said. I brought some music.

She had set up an iPod with speakers. She turned it on.

The music started. He heard a plinking piano and a woman's voice, raspy and clear at the same time.

Who is this?

It's Billie Holiday, she said.

I don't know who she is.

She's a singer. Was. A jazz singer.

She pulled down the sheet and touched his back. He listened closely to the music. He heard the scrape of the recording and the piano like rain and the voice lifted above the music like a kite jerking and soaring above the trees. Then the voice sang something about having a man and the sound of it changed and all of a sudden it was lively but desperate at the same time. He listened to the voice and the feeling behind the voice, the drops of piano rain falling, falling, and then what went on next in his brain and his body was a kind of revolution. The light in the dim room went dark with a few sparks of fire punctuating the black and the darkness swallowed him in a rapid monstrous grip and he felt a shot of pain dissecting him from his ribs up between his eyes and all of a sudden he could see his sleeve against the sequined fabric of a woman's dress and he heard the piano music speed up and swing and then the sound of trombones blew in and with the band came a car driving under streetlights along the park and the smell of coffee wafting from a pastry shop and he heard the plinking of the piano again it made him want to cry and there was the sound of the saxophone case clicking shut.

Is this okay? Do you want me to turn the music off?

He had twitched, or cried out, or said something.

Maybe I've heard this before. I didn't think so, but . . . He couldn't finish.

The streets were lit up at night and as he drove through them he saw the watercolor reds and greens wash over his hands through the windshield and he heard noises and felt feelings as if they were his memories, his feelings, but they were not and yet he knew this place, this night, and occasional sparks flew by in the black air which made no sense but which had to be accepted, as all of this had to be, the streetlights spilling a yellow-gold light, the line of cars shiny and bulked along the sidewalk, the excitement of the crowd outside, a woman's neck turning as he stepped out of the car. The memory was like an explosion and he was inside it, living through it and it surrounded him and slowly he breathed into it and found that it made him feel safe. This was where he was headed. He was entering someplace. It seemed to be his life.

A woman's hand slipped into his. The chips of mineral in the pavement glittered and seemed to float above the ground. The whole world glittered. It was cold out, a winter's night. He felt the air in his lungs. The woman's hand in his was warm. They joined the crowd on the sidewalk. They entered the throng. They stepped inside.

Milo reached for a hand and it was not there. He felt the wall and it was cold with a slight pattern of microscopic bumps. He was back in his room.

He did not remember coming back to his room or how he had gotten into bed. The nurse must have brought him. Honor usually said good-bye but maybe he had been too lost to the world to hear her. Or maybe his madness had shut her up. He was embarrassed by his crazy self. He knew he shouldn't be, least of all around her, she seemed so understanding. But the more she understood him the more he wanted to hide. What was he hiding? And how much did she know?

They never spoke about it, his stories. She would ask him what hurt, everything, what felt better this time, nothing, why wouldn't he let her work on his front, that was none of her fucking business only he didn't say it quite that way she was too nice and pretty and kind. Why did he deserve such kindness? Because he was one of the losers, he guessed. No legs that were any good, no real heroics to speak of, just dumb bad luck and now these wild imagined memories like he had been implanted with someone else's brain, real science fiction bullshit that he had never been interested in, not in his whole life. As a kid he had loved books, he still loved books, but stories of real people, or fake real people, not impossible, mystical things.

The bumps on the wall sharpened to his touch. He moved his hand and it was like touching sandpaper but worse, a thousand needles. This was the way the pain would conquer him, he thought. It would take over his body, then his mind, and then the outside world. When even Honor's hands hurt him, that's when it would all be over. Then it occurred to him that the story inside him was not actually painful. He felt free from pain when he was inside the story.

A black saxophone case came through the wall. It fell down on the end of his bed. It opened to reveal its gleaming instrument. Now it clicked shut again and he was holding it and he was walking with it swinging above a cobblestone street. A smell of coffee came wafting out of an Italian pastry shop. *She would have waited all day for him.* A woman's scarf slid onto the ground and when he walked into the pastry shop the voice of Billie Holiday was singing from the radio.

1936

Joe ordered a coffee and drank it with a lot of sugar. He was standing at the counter, it was a very authentically Italian pastry shop, and then he saw in the clean curving glass over the perfectly rendered pastries the reflection of a familiar pattern. She was standing next to him. She didn't see him and he thought he would drink his coffee and leave but then the words came out of his mouth anyway.

I recognize your scarf, he said.

She looked quickly at him, a little frightened. Then she recovered.

Not my face? she said.

That too, he said.

He went to law school in the neighborhood. Vivian was using the library nearby, researching graduate programs. Her father wanted her to get a certificate to teach. She wanted to paint, but her parents told her that that was only for rich girls. They sat at a little table on the sidewalk. They were in Greenwich Village. All kinds of people walked by. Women with artistic clothes, he thought, students, businessmen, foreigners. His saxophone case bounced against his leg as he nervously jiggled his foot. He was playing a gig tonight downtown and so he was not going straight home after his classes. He had some time. She would show him her favorite bookshop. He tossed some coins on the scuffed black table and they headed west.

The winding streets took them past shops where the awnings flapped a little in the October breeze and the lettering looked like it could have been written centuries ago. Old watches and silver trinkets on trays lined with velvet, men in aprons standing outside their stores with their hands on their hips, gloved bohemian ladies walking up steep stairs, entering arts clubs and shuttered parlors. Joe spent most of his time at the law school, not soaking up the atmosphere downtown, and now he looked around as if suddenly the wallpaper had come to life. In window boxes yellow flowers spilled overboard and fell to earth. A little cemetery waited secretly behind a wall. In back of the Jefferson Market was a garden whose tall dying blooms stuck out through the bars of a black gate. They passed restaurants that had to be entered by walking a few steps below sidewalk level. The tranquil streets were lined with row upon row of stoops leading up to town house after town house, worlds within private worlds. As they were drawn west the tree-lined passages surrendered glimpses of the river, light at the end of a tunnel. It was by the river that he had first come upon her.

He adored his wife and when he passed an antique shop and glanced in the window he thought of Pearl and what she would like as a gift. He saw diamond rings and hanging earrings and wanted to shower her with tokens of his deep, heartfelt, steadfast appreciation. He remembered the feeling of coming off of the ship and into her arms and the way she had held him with her smile. She was his shelter. He wanted to share life with her, to take her to hear the music he loved, especially Count Basie, a new bandleader out of Kansas City, whom he'd heard only on the radio. He'd seen an advertisement in the newspaper saying that

Basie and his orchestra would be making their New York debut on Christmas Eve at the Roseland Ballroom. He wanted to tell Pearl about it, but he was afraid that she would disapprove. She would say that they did not have the money. She would be right. She was sensible and her maturity extended to everything she did. He felt it in the way she held him tightly when he came home. He loved the strong familiar feeling of her touch. When he pictured Pearl and himself in his mind he saw them like two carved figures clasped in an embrace. He had known her for over thirteen years. They had met when they were very young. The feeling of his holding her and of her holding him was never far from his thoughts. He could not imagine his life without Pearl. But when he thought of the two of them holding each other close, he could not fail to notice that they weren't dancing.

Honor

You have hands like the hands of a shaman.

What does that mean? Some kind of healer?

Something like that. I heard about it from a guy who was in Vietnam. He comes to talk to some of us. His plane went down in Laos. He lived with the Hmong. He met a shaman.

Honor was putting on her coat. He didn't usually speak to her this much. He was still on the table. The nurse hadn't come yet.

He told us that shamans go on journeys and speak to the dead. They meet the people, the spirits who haunt the sick.

This guy said that to become shamans they usually had suffered an illness, or a traumatic injury.

She was winding her scarf around her neck.

Anything like that ever happen to you? he asked.

She kept winding her scarf.

No, she lied.

She stood there for a moment. She could still see the saxophone case. It was black leather and beat-up, with a metal lock that was slightly rusted from the ocean air. The handle was squarish with rounded corners and it fit snugly in a man's hand. Honor lifted her messenger bag and swung it over her shoulder. She could practically feel the weight of the heavy horn in its leather case.

An autumn sunset, the boats on the river. Joe was standing next to Vivian looking out at the water. They seemed to be drawn together to the water. Her hair blew around in the wind and it looked like someone kept lifting it up and putting it back down. Her eyes squinted into the colors. She was not wearing her sunglasses. Boats rolled by. She told him about Italy and seeing the paintings there that she had always admired in books. He had been to Italy too, once, for a couple of days before his ship had sailed home, but he had not looked much at the paintings. He remembered the sound of the language. The music in the mornings of people talking in the quiet streets. The cups and plates and voices and silver clattering in the cafes.

Joe felt the thrill of talking to someone who had also traveled, who liked music, who felt deeply about places. He could tell that Vivian knew the excitement of waking

up in an unknown room, of taking in the emptiness and
freedom of a wind-ripped sky at sea. She also loved cities:
the stink and beauty and business and nighttime of the city.
And she loved music. He broached the subject of music
gently, because he was afraid that they might disagree too
much about it and he would be crestfallen, but he was
wrong, or right to care, because they shared that too. They
both loved the wild sound coming east from the Midwest,
and the sultry energy of the music uptown. She did not
seem like someone who would understand it; she was elegant and intellectual and intimidating. But he didn't really
seem like he would understand it either. He might have
appeared too conventional, too tame. As it turned out she
was not too intellectual to feel it and he was not too conventional to understand. They loved the same music in the
same way: like they would die without it. Like they could
die from it.

She told him about a man, a distant relation on her
father's side, whose family had made cymbals in Turkey.
They were an Armenian family and now they made
cymbals for the jazz drummers in New York. They had
a secret formula for making cymbals that had come
from their ancestor, an alchemist in Istanbul in the seven-
teenth century. Joe laughed and said that he didn't believe
her. She said it was true. She would take him to meet
them.

Do you know the secret formula? he asked her.

Yes, she said, but I'll never tell.

When it was time to go he walked close to her and
the backs of their hands brushed. At the subway he offered to ride back to Brooklyn with her, he still had hours

before he was going to play, but she said that it wasn't necessary.

When it was time to say good-bye she looked away.

You never showed me the bookstore, he said.

No, she said. I guess I didn't.

CHAPTER THREE

Milo came wheeling in wearing bloodstained boots. She wouldn't have known it was blood but he told her.

Whose boots are they? Honor asked.

A dead man's, he said. Actually, two dead men. Me, and the guy who saved my life.

Pearl

They were smiling in the picture in the picture frame. It sat on a little table by the sofa. Pearl looked at the smiles and saw herself years younger, her happiness captured like a butterfly pinned and resurrected under glass. Joe was smiling too and his warm eyes stared out at the simple room, the doorway to the kitchen, and her. She felt the warmth of his presence even when he was not home. Just knowing he was around and not sailing across the ocean gave her peace of mind.

She was cleaning the living room although it was not dirty. She had already shopped for groceries and washed his clothes and taken the lamp that had broken in to be fixed and gone to the butcher who was her friend, it was important to make friends with the butcher. She had carried the heavy bags up their street, Featherbed Lane. It was called Featherbed Lane because during the Revolutionary War it had been lined with featherbeds to muffle the sound of marching soldiers. She didn't know anything about the battle, who had been fighting whom, or what they had been fighting for, but the anecdote gave a sense of history and romance to the otherwise dreary six-story building. It validated her feeling that important things would happen, were happening, for them in this apartment. Her cleaning was a kind of constant readying for this coming event. Her cleaning possessed a nearly spiritual anticipation. She had straightened up the desk in the living room where he studied for his law classes. She had stacked his books. She had put everything in its place.

The picture kept smiling. It had been taken on their wedding day, almost thirteen years ago, in the backyard of her parents' stucco house in Los Angeles. She had met Joe in the desert. She had met him as the result of an accident. It turned out to have been, for them, a happy accident. And now that she thought about it, her whole life since seemed like a happy accident, a random occurrence. How could she have met her husband, her soul mate, in such an unexpected way if it had not been Fate? It was only a matter of time before the meaning of that fateful event would be revealed to her. She had not always felt certain about things, but she had developed over the years, perhaps out of necessity, a fierce unwavering faith in her marriage and its rightness in the world. The picture kept smiling.

1923

At night, in her tent, Pearl switched on a small electric lamp and opened a letter that she had found in her pocket earlier that evening. She lay on an army cot, not her usual bed, and stretched out her legs. There were a few bugs circling around in the glare of the light and their shadows cast enormous winged demons on the canvas sides of the tent. Pearl was not easily frightened but she would have turned off the lamp to get rid of the insects if it had not been for the letter.

Go away, she said, to the bugs, to the shadows, to the empty tent.

The letter was addressed to "The Wardrobe Girl." There was no postmark—it had been slipped into her pocket like a reverse theft—and the handwriting was firm and clear, with a slight leftward slant. It was dated June 5, 1923.

Dear Miss Wardrobe Girl,

You probably have no notion of my existence, but I see you every day. And you see me. I am one of the Israelites.

I believe you took some notice of me yesterday when

you handed me my loincloth. I have green eyes. For-give me if I am mistaken. And please forgive my forwardness.

I long to speak to you. Will you meet me outside the gates of the city tomorrow morning at sunrise? I know you must wake up early, as we all do.

With Anticipation and Respect,
Solomon Eckstein

Pearl was eighteen years old and had never been in love. She'd had a sweetheart, a young man from the neighborhood who had an instinctive gift for the piano, but he didn't support her desire to have a career, and so they had parted ways amicably when he left for college and she went on to finish high school and follow her dream. She felt some sadness about the boy from time to time, when she sat alone in her parents' yellow kitchen late at night or when she saw a mother and child holding hands and felt a strange shiver of disappointment pressing against her ribs.

Mostly, however, she was too busy with work to think about men, and if she'd really thought about it she would have said that anyway she adored her job. This was accurate, but what she later came to realize was that she had gravitated to the line of work she was in, in large part because it continually held forth the promise of true love.

She walked to the gates at dawn. She passed rows of tents, storerooms, two huge mess tents, and an emergency hospital. Children were heading toward the large school tent. To the north, under a still twinkling sky, trainers and herders were starting their day of tending to more than two thousand animals. The entire city was waking up, and

Pearl felt the military purposefulness of people gathered for a common goal. As the last shreds of night were brushed away and a pink light lifted over the desert in waves, she breathed in deeply and stepped under the three-hundred-foot-high gate of the temple of Ramses II.

When she emerged, it occurred to her that she had no idea who she was waiting for. She had tried to remember a face with green eyes, but she had no memory of one. She stood in front of the exterior of the massive gate, which was sculpted with seated Egyptians and large horses and faintly anachronistic-looking wheels. Ahead of her stretched an enormous avenue of sand lined with twenty-four sphinxes. She looked tiny standing before the gate, like a plastic figurine from an aquarium or a dollhouse tossed onto a piece of human-sized furniture. It was cold. The sand began to blow around, covering her shoelaces and collecting in the folds of her socks and skirt and wool coat. She wore a pale blue scarf around her neck and now she took it off and tied it around her head. She felt ridiculous, but after a while she lost herself in the majesty of the double row of sphinxes, and beyond them, the distant unfixable line of the sea.

A man approached her. She didn't recognize him, but she was not disappointed. He was tall and wide-shouldered, with dark wavy hair. He was squinting against the blowing sand.

Mr. Eckstein? Pearl said.

No, no, he said quickly. I'm his friend. I met him on the train out here. My name is Joe. He held out his hand and they shook hands.

I don't understand, she said.

Solomon couldn't come. He's been injured. He was

helping overnight with the animals and something happened. Something with a horse. He was thrown.

Will he be all right? Pearl asked, finding herself deeply concerned about this man she didn't remember.

I don't know.

Pearl followed the stranger, without thinking about it, she later realized, to the emergency hospital. On the way, Joe explained that Solomon had told him at dinner the night before about the letter and the plan to meet in front of the gate, and that when Joe had heard of the accident he thought it was only decent to find her, The Wardrobe Girl, and tell her what had happened. He said all this while rushing through the men's half of the camp, nervously pulling her by the hand. The men's and women's camps were strictly separated because Mr. DeMille wanted absolutely no hanky-panky. There was even what was referred to as a Sex Squad on the location to scour the moonlit beaches at night. Mr. DeMille had seen affairs on set cause too many problems and he could not afford to have anything go wrong. Even the extras knew how far over budget this ambitious and difficult project was going, and rumors flew through the mess tent every night at dinner. It was said that just yesterday Mr. DeMille had been heard screaming into the telephone at one of the producers: "What do you think I'm making? 'The Five Commandments'?"

Solomon was asleep in the infirmary. Joe told the nurses that Pearl was Mr. Eckstein's beloved sister and so they let her in; skeptically, however, because Pearl did not look a thing like her brother. Solomon Eckstein was one of 225 Orthodox Jews that DeMille had insisted on casting for his epic. Advertisements had appeared in the daily press and a booth was set up in a vacant lot at the edge of downtown Los Angeles. In grave opposition to his parents' wishes, Solomon had eagerly applied for the job. He had always dreamt of being in pictures. Even if it meant becoming one of Pharaoh's slaves. Even if it meant shivering in the windy desert wearing nothing but a loincloth. Even if it meant being sprayed daily with gallons of glycerine to make it appear as if the Israelites were sweating. Each morning he submitted to being stripped and covered from head to foot in special oils which gave him the appearance of being almost black with sunburn.

And now here he was, passed out from a concussion. Pearl sat with him for over an hour, her hand resting on his. She talked to him about the infirmary. She told him that the nurses were taking good care of him. She brushed the hair out of his face.

That night, she went to hear Joe play saxophone with the thirty-piece Palm Court Orchestra of the Ritz-Carlton in New York. The band had been brought to the desert by DeMille for the purpose of inspiring the Israelites and the charioted army of Egypt during the Exodus. When it came time for the actual chase, a span of black thoroughbreds imported from Kansas City stampeded from the rear. Riderless horses headed for the band, which went on playing in evening dress until the moment they were ambushed, leaving broken instruments and shredded tuxedos scattered across the dunes. Sand swirled in the wreckage. Joe was unscathed, but Pearl always wondered if the same horse that had thrown Solomon had led the stampede. She never did get to see those green eyes.

Honor

You're scaring me with those boots, she said.

He was wearing them every day now.

They're just boots, Milo said.

Bloodstained boots, you said. The boots of a dead man. Two dead men.

He paused a moment.

I don't believe you're scared of anything, he said.

Honor was turning off the lights. She stopped, her hand on the switch.

What makes you say that?

Because you don't flinch.

What are you talking about?

You know what I'm talking about.

She didn't say anything.

Are you going to make me say it?

She couldn't say anything.

His hands were clenched now. His eyes were shut.

No, she said. No I'm not.

She turned off the light.

1923

Joe was able to visit her by night. In the evenings, the school was converted into a location for vaudeville acts and jazz and after he finished his last set, he would pack up his saxophone and walk with Pearl down the avenue of sphinxes, or along the well-patrolled but not completely policed beach. The moon was slender and shrouded in fog. They held hands in the darkness. They watched the black celluloid ripplings of the nearly invisible ocean. Joe pulled Pearl close to him to keep her warm.

In her tent, he scolded her for going to meet Solomon. What was she doing, he said, waiting at sunrise for a man she didn't know? He might have been dangerous.

If I hadn't gone to meet that man, she reminded him, I would never have met you.

After the parting of the Red Sea, during which Pearl had followed Mr. DeMille's strict instructions and rushed headlong into the waves with hundreds of others in order to retrieve seaweed and spread it around on dry sand so that it would look as if the ocean had just separated, Pearl agreed to go to New York with Joe. They stopped briefly in Los Angeles to tell her parents, who were relieved at the thought of their daughter settling down and getting out of the picture business, and who arranged the wedding quickly and modestly. They had a small house in a flat part of the city. The reception was held in their minuscule yard. Pearl later remembered her wedding day as the image of a palm shadow on a tablecloth. The image was captured for eternity in the background of the picture in her living room. Their honeymoon was a ride on a comfortable train east. By the time *The Ten Commandments* opened at the George M. Cohan theater in New York that December, Pearl could navigate her new city like a native, and she and Joe were expecting their first child.

The doctors didn't have any answers, he said.

What? Honor said.

Milo's eyes were closed. He had a look on his face, even with his eyes closed, like he was trying to remain calm, as though he were keeping some great pain at bay. It reminded her of an animal working away at a wound with a perfectly composed expression.

They never figured out what was wrong, he said.

The doctors here? What are you talking about?

Every year for five years Pearl lost a baby.

Honor stopped asking questions.

I'm sorry, she said.

There was always a lot of blood.

I'm very sorry, she said.

He was still talking with his eyes closed. Now it was like a statue talking, or a ghost.

We wanted a child so much, he said. It was hard to see her sad. She was very brave.

Very brave, Honor said.

You have to understand, he said, there was a lot of blood.

Then his face twisted into a horrible mask, like one of those monstrous inflatable Halloween masks, and then as if someone had pulled a string, the face folded and slowly collapsed into itself like some airless and decomposing plant.

I understand, she said.

She couldn't tell him that she didn't understand. That she wanted desperately to know if his pain was for the story he was telling her or for his own hidden story, which he wouldn't tell her.

Either way, she supposed it didn't really matter. She felt the sadness in him and it hung around her shoulders and when she left he was resting and calm again and she very quietly closed the door.

At the nurses' station they were talking about recipes and global warming. The lights were low and on a desk there were cups of soda and a sandwich. Honor recognized most of the nurses by now, some of them she had come to know a little. She looked over at them while she waited for the elevator. Then one of them said, What is it? You don't look so good. Honor came over and sat down.

She took off her bag. Her long hair swung. Her coat grazed the linoleum floor.

He seems like he's getting worse, she said.

They all get worse, one of them said. Then sometimes they get better. She put her cup down and turned a page of the newspaper.

I'm not sure I'm helping him.

Can't be sure, another one said. Even if you think you are helping, it could just be God's work.

Three of the four of them nodded.

But sometimes I think I'm even hurting him, that the work I do causes him pain.

That can happen. Nothing so bad about pain.

Honor's eyes widened a tiny amount at this remark as

she took it in. The nurse who said it glanced back down at her newspaper, with a shadow of a smile that showed that she was pleased to share some of her wisdom.

Do any of you ever see things when you take care of patients? Or hear things?

Everyone has stories.

He seems to have a lot of stories, Honor said.

She was leaning forward now, searching for help.

He's been through a lot, one of the nurses said.

Honor leaned forward more.

Do you know what? she asked them, scanning their faces. I mean, do you know what he's been through?

They were quiet for a moment and then one of them said:

You look like you've seen something.

I have.

She sat there in her coat and scarf, looking at them. She had the distant benevolent gaze of an angel in a painting. But her skin was ashen and it looked like it had been stretched across her skull. Her hair was unwashed. Her hands were bones.

Try not to let it frighten you.

Okay, she said.

You should get home and get some rest.

Okay.

One of them walked her back to the elevator and pressed the button. Honor looked at the oily smears of fingerprints on the metal plate around the buttons and thought that she might be sick. Inside while she was making the short descent, she had to sit down on the floor of the elevator so that she wouldn't fall down.

CHAPTER FOUR

They met on the steps of the Museum of Natural History. Vivian had never been there and Joe was stunned when she told him because he knew that she had grown up in New York City. I like looking at art not at animals, she had said. He had told her that these animals were works of art, or interesting specimens anyway, and it was a good place to meet. He waited in the wind. He sat down on a step. He thought she might not come. He wouldn't blame her for not coming. He shouldn't be there himself. He should be studying in the library. People walked up and down the steps with intention and meaning. Children ran. It was late October and the sky was darkening over the park, quickly, like a bright face turning away to show only a head of falling tresses. The orange and yellow leaves on the trees were shadowed and what had looked golden in the sun now seemed thinner and more tissue-like, papery, not as real although actually more so. He had the newspaper with him but he didn't read it. It stuck straight up out of his jacket pocket. He decided to stand. He stretched his legs. He walked to the top of the stairs. He gazed north.

She surprised him from the other direction. She came up behind him and said his name. It sounded different when she said his name because now she knew him and he could hear it in her voice.

In the Akeley Hall of African Mammals, which had just recently opened, people stood rapt in front of the dioramas of bongos and mandrills and impalas. They peered into the meticulously reconstructed alternate worlds and seemed to be transported through space. They were still wearing their hats and gloves. Children pressed their hot faces against the glass and the guards kindly told them to step back but it was hard for the children to understand why they could not walk inside, in the wild. Joe identified with the children; he wished he could enter other worlds. Vivian stopped and dutifully admired the taxidermy and detail but she could not pretend that she felt anything. Joe looked at her while she looked at the rain forests and savannahs and he thought that it would be beautiful to see her in those locations under a real moon, a living sun. He could sense that she didn't really care for any of it, but she was not unkind and said that he was right, it was interesting. They walked around and around the elephants.

I can picture you in any of these places, he said. India, Burma, Siam.

I'd love to go, she said. But I can't say I feel like I've been there from coming here.

I can tell.

I'm sorry.

Don't be sorry. I thought you would like it but I was wrong. I'm wrong about a lot of things.

He dug his hands into his pockets and looked down at the shiny marble floor.

Like what? she asked.

Hmm, he thought. He lifted his head and gazed up at the ceiling. When he had come up with an answer he brought his head down, quickly glanced at her with a brief smile, and then looked straight ahead.

Like how to earn a living, he said. I don't want to be a lawyer. You know that.

But you're being practical. That's not wrong.

You don't seem concerned about being practical.

That doesn't make me right.

You seem right to me.

They had walked out of the hall and were heading down a dim corridor. She had a little bounce in her gait that he hadn't noticed before, like a tiny dance step in between strides. It was graceful and somewhat aristocratic. Her long coat was cinched at the waist and it swayed a bit with every step.

Are you at all practical? he asked. I mean, do you worry about everyday things? You seem so calm and unconcerned.

Of course I worry. My father is at home dying.

Now it was her turn to gaze downward, at the shiny floors, the places where their feet clicked and sent out echoes.

I'm sorry. That's very difficult. I know you worry about him. I meant little things. The details of life.

She stopped and looked at him.

There's not much I can do about them, is there?

Her eyes were forming a question and he wanted her to ask it but she didn't. When she started walking again she said:

You said Pearl might be joining us. Is she coming?

No, no she couldn't.

I see.

They were entering the Hall of Asian Mammals. The hall had been open for several years and he knew it well. He had liked to come here and stroll around with Pearl. They had stopped doing it after a while because it was a place filled with children. Now he didn't notice the children. He and Vivian stood in front of the water buffalo not looking at it.

This used to be a special place for me and Pearl.

That must be nice, to share special places.

It is. It was.

At one time he would have rattled off all of his thoughts to Pearl about the buffalo, the water, the filigreed fish he thought he could see in the stream, the pitch of the cries of the children when they stopped and laughed in front of the gorilla diorama, the tragicomic echoing sound of those cries bursting into the otherwise hushed atmosphere like sounds heard in a real forest, a real desert. But now he did not say just anything.

Is there anyone, anyone special in your life right now? He was gazing intently at the buffalo's habitat.

That's a hard question, she said. Yes and no.

When she said yes and no he heard yes.

Pearl and I would love to meet him, he said.

There was a stillness between them.

You know him, she said.

He understood what she meant.

In front of the Siberian tiger he took her hand. Her face was suspended in the window glass and it looked like the tiger was crying.

Honor

I'm sorry I couldn't talk about it the other day.

Talk about what? Milo said.

Talk about this, about what happens here.

I forgive you, he said. I don't want to talk about it either.

He clenched and unclenched his fist. Then he said: You might have heard from the people around here, I don't really want to talk about anything.

But you talk to me.

Not much.

Sometimes in your sleep.

He twisted his head as far as he could and cocked an eyebrow at her from the table.

Is that right?

Yes, that's right.

I thought it was all . . . unspoken.

Not completely.

So what do I say?

Crazy stuff. Some scary things. Some things that make no sense.

Sounds like me.

But it doesn't sound like you. It's your voice but it's like you're in character, someone else. You talk about things like you're there. In the past.

You must think I'm a lunatic.

I don't.

She rubbed more oil into her hands and put her fingers on his neck.

I like it, she said. I like your stories.

His head shook a little in her hands when he laughed.

Well that makes you the lunatic.

Maybe, she said.

We both are, he said.

That sounds about right.

Have you told anyone about any of this?

No, not anyone.

Don't. They'll either put me on a shitload more medication or they'll say you've lost your mind and fire you.

You wouldn't like that.

No, I wouldn't like that.

Then I won't tell anyone.

Thanks.

She had her hands on his arm.

So, no stories today? she asked.

Nope. Why don't you tell me one? You never tell me anything about yourself.

You never ask.

That's not true. I did once.

She thought of what she might tell him and then decided against it. They were quiet for a long time.

You know, you're helping me, he said.

How can you tell?

Because I want to know what's going to happen next.

I guess that's called having something to live for, she said. I'm glad to hear it.

And she was. She was smiling.

Maybe one of these days you'll tell me something about yourself.

Maybe, she said.

She would sit and think about whatever she had seen with him as she rode home on the subway. Sometimes she listened to her iPod while she thought. This was the time in her life when she listened to music to save herself. Her music and her soldier's stories, they kept her from falling apart. The sounds wound around her like gauze. She'd had a friend, someone she didn't talk to anymore, and he had given her a book by Ralph Ellison about jazz. It said: In those days, we could either live with music or die with noise, and we chose, somewhat desperately, to live.

The iPod sat in her lap. She realized that the music had stopped some time ago and that she had just been sitting with the earphones in and no sound. At her stop she got out and walked home down the uncrowded streets to her walk-up. She felt less and less as though she lived in her small apartment and more as if the hospital uptown were her home. The time between her visits to her soldier seemed as though it was not her real life. She saw other clients, worked some days in a doctor's office, took classes, had her friends. But she found that she had to remind herself of who she was and sometimes riding on the train or walking down the street she would tell herself: You are Honor. You are twenty-one. You are not a dancer, anymore. You live alone.

The time she spent with Milo was now becoming something of its own secret. At first she told some friends about him, the mysterious soldier who wouldn't lie on his back. But why not? they would ask. What's wrong with him? What happened to him? Why didn't she know? Why didn't she ask him? Then they became bored and talked of other things. There were relationships, films, jobs, people moving in different directions, changing lives. But she was not concerned with any of those things anymore. Some of her friends were worried about her. She had changed. Was she doing okay? She said she was but really being okay or not okay was not important to her anymore. Being okay seemed like a state of mind from another life. Her old life was as insignificant to her now as a passing shadow she had stepped across yesterday, or a lost scrap of conversation overheard. She could not remember her old life. She could not think about the person she had been. She was thinking about her soldier.

There was a woman swaying underwater, her black hair wafting weightlessly like ink. The woman became a tree. The trees were moving in the darkness. It was evening when they left the museum and walked down the steps and saw the park.

They were not holding hands. They walked quietly west. Joe said he felt like he was forever walking her to the subway. Forever saying good-bye.

That's really all we can say to each other, she said.

Don't say that, he said.

I don't want to be angry with you for the way things are, she said. Don't be angry with me.

I couldn't be.

You could, she said. But don't be. I was just being honest.

The stately buildings along the street were turning purple now and their stoic faces gazed out gravely at the ornate hulk of the museum. They were a bastion of traditional values, of responsibility and discipline and order. They seemed to be broadcasting that it was time to go home. People should be inside now, having dinner, sitting with families. Joe hunched a little under the heavy shadows.

We have to say good-bye, she said. This really isn't possible.

His face was right up next to hers. She was in his shadow now.

I know, he said. Then he whispered: I know. Let's just keep saying good-bye.

CHAPTER FIVE

Summer came. She had first encountered Milo in late winter and now it was summer. In the stifling heat the city seemed to empty out and become desolate, then explode from the stagnating hotness and open itself up like some vulgar dying flower. On the sidewalks, garbage cooked in the cans and in the gutters. Fat water bugs cruised the pavement with abandon. People wore very few clothes. Honor opened the windows of her tiny walk-up apartment and brought out fans. The edges of the large piece of fabric thrown over the sofa rippled in the warm breeze. The Rolling Stones played in her kitchen, as they had played in her mother's kitchen and possibly, if perhaps only by accident, in her grandmother's. The music, overloaded with memories and associations and familiar melodies, sounded cheerfully timeless and not the least bit irreverent. The band played valiantly through the heat. It went banging on like some workhorse Dixieland band at a Fourth of July gathering on a town green.

It was, in fact, the Fourth of July. Honor whistled along to the tunes and felt oddly patriotic, as if these songs were her own private national anthem. When that was over she put on some Billie Holiday and felt more deeply connected to her country, and this time she didn't whistle along because she didn't want to miss hearing the words. For dinner she had prepared a traditional barbecue of wheat-free pasta and seaweed salad with a little bit of this morning's leftover French toast for dessert. She was not really hungry. Her mother's birthday had been July Fourth and she remembered year after year of celebratory cakes. Now she was not in touch with Anna, and so the day had a painful undercurrent of independence. But she would go up onto her roof later to watch the fireworks. They were the only part of the holiday that really interested her. She especially liked small-town fireworks, the kind that shot up only a little ways and gently drooped when they fell like handkerchiefs thrown in surrender. Big-city fireworks were staggering and awesome, but terrifying in their resemblance to real bombs bursting in air. The wheels of whirling fire setting the skyline aflame. Great explosions of unnatural red thunder. A simple constellation of white stars expanding into gigantic webbed galaxies of light.

The night air was still sweaty when she emerged from the building staircase onto the black roof. A few people were milling around, waiting for the festivities to begin, holding cups and beer bottles. She said hello but hung off to the side. She did not really know her neighbors. Then the sky lit up and the world appeared to be taking a picture of itself. There was a lengthy flash as if from an old-fashioned camera and the population stood frozen in the moment, holding their smiles, waiting for their transformation. When it was all over there was that minute of uncertainty about whether or not it was really all over and then a general agreement as to the appropriate timing and amount of applause. The night was still hot. Nothing had changed. As people filed back down the staircase Honor walked to the edge of the roof and lifted her face to the breeze. At the edge of the roof she had a quick memory of someone sitting on the edge of a roof, and then it passed. She turned her intense gaze on the dark cityscape and thought about her soldier.

Her soldier: that was how she thought about him now. Her soldier who had begun to tell her his secrets. He spoke to her through his body and she felt as though if she could piece together his stories, she could piece together the person. The person: Milo Hatch, formerly of Penobscot, Maine. Milo Hatch, who had suffered a spinal cord injury in the desert and that was all he would say about it. Milo Hatch, a handsome young man, only in this story, the story that she was receiving from him, he was not a twenty-four-year-old war veteran struggling for his sanity in the first decade of a new century, he was a young jazz musician in New York in the 1930's who was falling in and out of love. And he was more: he was the boats on the Hudson River at sunset, the blue light of a September dusk, a black car pulling up to a gritty curb at night, a woman with ships in her eyes. He was leading her someplace, pulling her into his memories as if he were taking her by the hand. Her hands on him. His stories moving through her. She didn't care if none of it seemed possible. It wasn't possible, but it was true.

Do you think he really loves her?
Who?
Joe.
I don't know, Milo said. What do you think?
His eyes were closed. She was working on his hand. He opened his eyes and looked up at her from his most peripheral vision. They were a soft shade of slate blue with flecks of yellow. His hair, she had never really noticed his hair before, it was brown and fell over his eyes when he looked downward. She felt grateful that he had taken her question seriously. She had been afraid to ask. She had told herself that she would not be the one to talk about it first but she had gone ahead and asked him anyway. He was looking at her, waiting for her, and she could not keep silent.
Honor said: I think he loves them both.

1969

One day the story changed. It could happen that way, just like life. There was a new character, a new era, the passage of time. There was the smiling picture from Pearl's living room but now the picture was in a different room, lying face up on top of a pile of papers and pictures and books. The frame was tarnished. The pile was too high, nearly teetering, and it sat under a desk shoved out of the way, one of those piles nobody wants to claim. On the desk were spread out contact sheets of black and white photographs and Kodachrome slides scattered like shells on a beach. Across the room a larger desk sat also covered with photographs and cameras and rolls of film in their canisters. The room turned out to be most of an entire apartment, a tiny one-bedroom in a brownstone. An ornate marble mantel at one end, two extravagant windows overlooking a city garden, a kitchenette tucked into the corner. Off the main room a small bedroom big enough for only a bed. A flowered sheet tacked up as a curtain. It felt like an office and it was a studio of a sort but you could also sense that someone lived there: the dirty dish on the table, the glass of water left on the mantel, a dress sprawled across the white foam of unmade sheets.

A door closed. You couldn't really see the woman but she walked quickly downstairs four steep flights and opened the front door—the sun came breaking in and then she emerged into the street like an actress stepping onstage. The bustle of commerce and society traipsed past as if it had been choreographed for her this sunny morning in May. The woman was in her fifties but looked younger, attractive, independent, you could tell from her determined posture and no wedding ring. She wore a dress but you could also tell that that was because she was going someplace important not because she wore a dress every day. Her hair was dark brown nearly black and she'd had it done and it fell smoothly nearly to her shoulders and she wore a headband because people did at the time, even older women. She carried a pocketbook with a small handle. Across the street from her stood a young woman perhaps in her early thirties who appeared to be watching the woman coming out of the brownstone. The older woman did not notice the younger woman. The older woman looked at her watch and walked toward the bus stop.

She waited for the bus. The bus stop was in front of a cake shop called the Jon Vie Bakery and she looked in the window of the shop at the cakes. There was a cake on display that looked like a doll wearing an enormous skirt. There was a real doll at the center of the cake sticking up from it and then the skirt was baked all around her in a dome shape. From time to time little girls would be drawn to the window and would pull their mothers over and point out the cake. The woman with the pocketbook smiled at the mothers in acknowledgment of the little girls' joy. The little girls' shadows fanned out on the side walk and bent up the side of the bakery and stopped where the window began. Real life stopped where the window began. The woman tilted her head and took it all in and saw the angle at which the girls pulled on their mothers' arms and how the shapes of the girls' hands echoed the shapes of the cookies in the display next to the cake and how the black shadows bending up toward the shop looked like broken people trying to climb inside. She tilted her head the other way and studied the pull of the girls' hands on the mothers' arms as they tried to draw them into the bakery and then the gravity of the mothers' strength as they directed the girls back down the street and into their day. The lines of the arms were interesting to the woman. They formed odd intersections and awkward angles.

Her bus came. It moved stealthily up Sixth Avenue like some slow methodical beast. She enjoyed watching the people arrive and depart and she furrowed her pretty brow and screwed up her expression as she took in everything about them: flat shoes, high boots, narrow pants that had come into fashion, thin ties that were last year's style, but more than clothes she observed the physical interactions between the people, the way a woman leaned forward toward a man who hung back, the tilt of a head as it responded to a question. Most of all she watched the children. Their feet dangled from the bus seats like branches waving above a pond, seeming to reach downward but then kicked back and forth by an invisible wind. Their mouths grimaced when they wanted to grimace. They squirmed when sweaters were buttoned up. They knelt backwards on the seat to look out the windows. They played with cards, jacks, balls, pennies strewn on an empty seat. They stared at nothing with their pink mouths open. Sometimes, they stared at her.

She got off. She turned a corner and walked up a block toward Fifth Avenue. In the middle of the block she entered a building. It was the Museum of Modern Art. Upstairs she met with a man in his office. He told her how excited they were to be presenting her work. He held out his hands and clasped them both around her small one. He said it would be a triumphant show. He strode through galleries and showed her where her pictures would be hung. The woman held tightly to her pocketbook. She was proud but also nervous. This museum in which she had spent so many warm happy hours since childhood now seemed vast and cavernous and cold. She wondered how her photographs would feel up on its walls. Her photographs had feelings in her mind. She felt for the first time a maternal concern about exposing them to the world. She had shown her pictures before but never in such a grand setting. Still, she was very proud.

The curator and two benefactors of the museum took her out to lunch in midtown. There were murals on the walls of the restaurant. She had a glass of wine. She had another. The curator had more. He said, of course she was justly famous for her black-and-white pictures but that to be honest he preferred the new color work. Less arty. Everyone ordered. She asked for the Dover sole, a specialty of the house, and handed the thick red leather menu back to the waiter. She looked at the pattern of the silver. She had worked with famous photographers and now one of the benefactors asked her about the famous men. There had been talk that she had had an affair with one of them and it was obvious that that was what the benefactress was implying and trying to verify with her questioning. The woman had the entitled air of the wealthy and privileged without the tact or discretion and she pretended not to notice that the person she was speaking to did not want to answer. It went on this way. The rich woman's mouth pursed before she took a sip of her drink. The rings on her fingers looked like enormous winged insects refracted through the crystal of her highball glass. Finally she said: I can see why you never married. You don't want to reveal anything. At this point the curator noticed what was happening and deflected the conversation with a detailed description of some remarkable new acquisitions. The woman photographer stared at the murals on the walls and had another glass of wine.

While the photographer was out the younger woman who had been watching her on the street rang all the buzzers on the front entrance of the small building. One old woman answered and let her in. The young woman had dark straight pretty hair, almost black, cut to just below her chin. It swung a tiny bit as she spoke to the old woman because she was shaking slightly. Her heart was beating very fast and she realized at once that this guileless old lady would answer any question. When asked where there might be a key to the top-floor apartment, the old woman said she had a spare one in case her neighbor was locked out. The old woman was wearing a housecoat and had liner scrawled madly around her eyes. It did not occur to her that this respectable-looking person in her late twenties or so might not be telling the truth when she said that the upstairs neighbor whom she called by name was her relative and that she had said that she could use the apartment but that she had forgotten to leave the key. So the old woman gave her the key. Her hand was bony like a bird's skeleton. The younger woman walked up to the top floor. The banister wobbled. Some of the poles along the stairway were missing. Above the top-floor landing a dirty skylight let in some dirty sun. She turned the key in the lock and the door opened and she stepped inside.

1936

On a corner not far from the Museum of Natural History Joe was holding Vivian in his arms. There was a wind in his hair and it blew forward onto her face and her hair blew around in his.

CHAPTER SIX

Saigon

The woman with the dark pretty hair who had lied to get the key to the photographer's apartment was sitting in the back of a hot room. She looked a few years younger. She was wearing a summer dress and she was pregnant. Her dark hair was longer and pulled back into a ponytail. Tiny beads of sweat filigreed her back and upper chest and she was fanning herself with an envelope. In the front of the room a list of charges against her husband was being read out loud and he was standing with his back to her. The room was small and crowded and out a tiny high window she could see the spinal arc of a curving palm frond. They were in Saigon. He had been flown from Soc Trang for the court-martial.

They were altering one of the charges. The charge that her husband, a physician, had failed to conduct himself as a medical officer and a gentleman was being changed to reflect that he was now being accused of having presented erroneous factual data to a general. He was also on trial for two other alleged violations of military law: One accused him of having presented an undisciplined appearance by not shaving and not wearing his uniform. The other accused him of having feigned mental illness while on duty.

Someone was called to testify. A young man in uniform sat in the front of the room and said that he had seen Captain Michaels out of uniform near the hospital in South Vietnam. Under cross-examination he said that on occasion the doctor's uniform had been missing buttons when he reported for physical training in the combat zone. The specialist was thanked for his testimony. More witnesses were called. They spoke to the merits of the accusation that Captain Michaels had approached the United States commander in Vietnam while the general was inspecting the hospital and had complained about a shortage of supplies. Captain Michaels had said that the shortages were of a kind that meant the difference between life and death. According to testimony, the general had said that he would look into the alleged shortages but that he had no sympathy for "whiners." Captain Michaels had received orders returning him to Saigon on the same day.

The light outside the tiny window turned the palm frond a dark gray. Captain Michaels's wife continued to fan herself in the July heat. The ink on the envelope smudged and bled from the moisture of her fingers. They called an army nurse. The nurse said that she had seen Captain Michaels performing his duties while out of uniform. She added that it was not unusual for officers, even the detachment commander, to wear civilian clothes while on duty. Then the commander was called to the stand, a major. He was questioned about his order to Captain Michaels to shave off a budding goatee. The major, who had a neat mustache, said that he had not cared for captain Michaels's goatee and that he had ordered him to shave it off. The captain had done so. Then he told the court that the captain had failed to salute on more than one occasion. The final witness was a specialist who said that many officers and enlisted men did not adhere to uniform regulations. The palm frond turned purple and then nearly black in the fading light. Captain Michaels's wife continued to fan herself until the proceedings were concluded for the day.

2005

I'm thinking what the hell is going on, he said.

Yes, she said.

Do you know what's happening?

He had pushed himself up onto one elbow and the sheet fell down to his waist. His chest was muscular and squared like the surface of a huge chessboard. The round of his shoulder that she knew so well by touch looked entirely different from this angle, too large to hold on to, something cut from stone.

I don't. I thought maybe you could tell me.

Who are they, these new people? He said it as if the others were familiar to him and not as much figments and ghosts as these new visions.

I think one of them is a photographer. The older one. And then the younger woman seems to be married to that army guy.

I got that, but who are they?

Milo, you know as much as I do.

It was the first time she had said his name. All I know is that these stories seem to be inside you. And that somehow when I touch you they come out. If you let us keep going maybe we can get some answers. But maybe not, she said.

He smiled at her.

So we're the blind leading the blind.

So to speak, she said.

He rolled back onto his chest and spread his arms out like wings. The muscles in his back where his wings would have attached rippled like water under wind. He splayed out his fingers and she thought that he might fly off the table.

Okay, he said. Bring it on.

All around Joe and Vivian it was getting dark. Glowing white lights were arriving in the streetlamps and in the windows of the buildings.

Do you know what we're doing? she said.

There were high trees along the sidewalk and the October wind that was blowing in her hair blew through the trees and seemed like it would blow out all the lights.

Iris

They moved the trial to New Orleans. The heat was just as bad. In the new courtroom Iris fanned herself with the newspaper. The story was all over the papers. It had started, probably, with a newspaper. She had been upset. He was gone. She was expecting their first child. He was drafted from the reserve. He was supposed to stay in Saigon. There were other doctors there who were regular army doctors but they were not sent to Soc Trang and he was.

Why was he sent instead of them? That's what she wanted to know. But no one would tell her. She wrote letters to her senators. She wrote to the Army Surgeon General's office. She was alone in New York and he was in South Vietnam. She was upset. It was perfectly understandable. But nobody understood. No one would tell her why.

The letters she received back on official stationery did not explain why her husband had been sent and not the army doctors and although the stilted words tried to convey sympathy for her situation they mentioned that many other wives were in the same position. Many hardships were necessary during wartime. Iris held the letter against her belly and closed her eyes. She was not an idiot. She was not a child. She knew that she was not alone in her misfortune. Did that make it any less unfair? Her husband was a reserve doctor. They had not bargained for this. She took out the heavy black manual typewriter in its case from the closet. Her back ached and she nearly dropped it on the floor. It was the one that he had had in medical school but she had always done most of his typing. As soon as she had finished an essay of her own she would roll in a fresh piece of rough paper for him. The sound of their marriage was the sound of typing, an uneven marching beat that unwittingly foreshadowed his uneven military career. He had no dreams of advancement in the army. He just wanted to help people, and at this rate to stay alive. But now here he was being court-martialed for nothing and she was worried that it would ruin his medical career. And that it was her fault.

Was it her fault? The newspaper. After the letters to the senators and the surgeon general went nowhere she had sent a letter to the editor. Of a major newspaper. In it, she had said that the secretive nature of the conduct of this war was unconscionable. She said that national security was a smokescreen the government was hiding behind to prevent the truth from being known. The letter was printed. There was a feeling among Captain Michaels's family and friends and associates that in spite of his own casual and critical behavior in Soc Trang it was this letter more than anything else that had resulted in his court-martial. His mother did not come to New Orleans for the trial. His father, who owned a pharmacy in Reading, Pennsylvania, had flown in and was sitting next to his daughter-in-law. But he did not look over at her during the proceedings. Sometimes she thought he had forgotten, happily, that she was there.

She was listening to the testimony about Captain Michaels's missing buttons from his uniform when the baby kicked for the first time.

Honor

Tomorrow's his birthday.

What?

Your friend. He turns twenty-five tomorrow.

Honor was standing at the nurses' station reading the paper. Her hair was undone and fell in a curtain shielding her face. She pulled it aside and looked at the nurse.

Do you think he would like a cake? she asked.

Everyone likes a cake.

Can he have one? Can I bring one in for him?

The nurse checked his chart. He's allowed to eat anything. He has physical therapy until eleven tomorrow. Then occupational therapy. Why don't you come in around lunchtime.

Will he be in our room? I won't have enough for everyone. And he wouldn't want a party anyway. We should be alone.

I'll get him there.

He'll probably hate it.

He hates a lot of things. Doesn't mean we should let him get away with it.

Honor flipped the pages of the paper.

He trusts me a little now. I don't want him to think I'm pushing it.

The nurse slid the paper over to her side of the counter. She started reading.

Don't forget to bring a candle, she said.

1936

It was late when Joe came home. He had been studying, he said. He had an exam. I know, she said, as if he'd already told her. She had dinner waiting for him and they sat at the little table in the kitchen. She had pot roast, his favorite, and string beans and roasted potatoes. No matter how little money they had she always managed to feed him well. She watched him while he ate and she seemed to enjoy just the movement of his jaw, the way he held his fork, the way he organized the remnants on his plate.

He closed his eyes when he took a sip of water.

I saw that bandleader you like is coming at Christmas.

Oh really? he said.

It was advertised in the paper.

He kept eating.

I thought we might go, she said.

He kept eating.

Then he said: Isn't it too expensive?

Yes, she said, it is. But I thought we deserved some fun.

It's very expensive, he said.

She stood up and took his plate.

If you think so, she said, scraping the plate.

No, no, he said, leaning back in the chair. Maybe you're right. He smiled. Maybe we should go.

.

They dismissed the charge of feigning mental illness. They refused to withdraw the two remaining charges. Then they called Captain Michaels as a witness.

The Captain testified in a calm voice. He responded to all of the accusations with reasonable defenses. Yes, he had complained but not because he wanted to be sent home. Yes, he had said there was a lack of vital surgical tools on the base. In fact, the shortages had proven on more than one occasion to be fatal in the operating room. Yes, he had let his facial hair grow, but when he returned to base, his commanding officer had ordered him to shave and he had.

He answered all of their questions and sat down. When he said fatal, his voice had faltered in a way that only his wife noticed. As he walked back to his seat, he made sure not to catch her eye.

The seven-man board deliberated for less than an hour. When they returned with a verdict Captain Michaels's wife was still sitting in the heat. The perspiration bloomed in large spots across the back of her dress. The head of the board gave the verdict. The verdict was guilty of conduct unbecoming an officer. The sentence was dismissal from the army. Captain Michaels was also convicted of a lesser charge of failing to shave, thereby presenting an undisciplined appearance. When the decision was read Captain Michaels showed no sign of emotion. According to the newspaper accounts, his pregnant wife who sat behind him in the courtroom showed signs of strain.

2005

The cake was vanilla with chocolate icing. Honor had stayed up late baking it. She used a mix from the health food store but still it took her a long time. She double-checked every instruction and ingredient. She made the icing.

She carried it on a plate and covered it with tinfoil. She leaned it against her body when she pushed open the door. He wasn't there yet and she set it out on the table. She put a candle next to it. She took off her coat and left the room to wash her hands. When she came back he was there, early, sitting in his wheelchair.

What is this? he said.

A cake, she said.

What for?

I heard it was your birthday.

He closed his eyes and rolled his head and his hair moved and he made a disgusted gesture with his mouth.

So this is a party? he said.

Not exactly. Not a party. I just thought it would be nice to celebrate.

She tilted her head. She bit her lip. She felt afraid of him for the first time.

You and your pity.

It's not pity. Look, if you don't want the cake we don't have to have it.

She walked over to take the cake away and he slammed it off the table with the back of his hand. The plate broke.

See that? he said. That's you, he said. You think you're so good but you're just using me to feel good. You and these goddamned stories. What do they have to do with me anyway? You're just some crazy lady with a fucked-up need to mess around in my head. You can just forget about it. I don't need this kind of help.

Okay, she said. She was looking at the cake on his arm. It was like pieces of flesh stuck all over.

So we understand each other? he said. This is all over, right? Because I don't know what it is you've been doing to me but I'm better off without it.

I wish you'd give it another try, she said. She was scared of him now but so scared that she felt she could say anything.

He pushed over the whole table. It dropped on its side like a fallen horse. They both looked at it for a long time.

I'm sorry about the cake, she said.

IIis eyes looked hurt like a boy's. They squinted up at her with a blue fire.

It's not the cake, he said. It's you.

PART TWO

Come sail your ships around me
And burn your bridges down.
We make a little history, baby,
Every time you come around.

—NICK CAVE, *"The Ship Song"*

CHAPTER SEVEN

They lived happily ever after. Anna gave birth to a baby girl at the tender age of seventeen and it was the beginning of a great love story. She had never known such joy. The round head burst forth from her like a marvelous idea. Her body shook with the revelation of new life. Her family, however, did not share the same attitude, and so the baby was taken from her and given to a respectable and grateful couple who were waiting anxiously outside the delivery room. It seemed that everything was right again with the world, except to Anna. Her father and mother handed the child over with a mixture of pride and revulsion. Pride and revulsion were popular sentiments in the late twentieth century. Ronald Reagan was president. For years, people had believed in believing in things, and when they went as planned the entire nation took credit; when they didn't, the country blamed someone else. But ever since the Vietnam War some people had started blaming themselves for things that did not go right, and because it was so unlike the national character to do so, an element of self-hatred had crept into the culture. On the streets you saw young people with hairstyles like a crown of fangs. The music blaring from enormous boxes sounded menacing and deranged. A lot of people wore black. It was also a very innocent time. Telephones were heavy and stayed at home. Sometimes they had buttons. Girls waited by the phone, literally. Boys did not dream of owning their own jet. Women who were not even old looked old. There was plenty of drug addiction, but not a lot of rehab. There was no Ecstasy. There were no antidepressants. There was no global village. There was no Internet. On the day that Anna gave birth to her daughter the sun was shining. Out the hospital window the East River flowed past like one long silver muscle, the way it had when Walt Whitman had mused over it in the preceding century, and like it would look to the passengers of a plane flying low over the city in the next century. Anna cried. She was too young and inexperienced to have truly maternal feelings yet, but the emotion she felt for her new baby was an uplifting, cosmic, unbounded passion. Her father, a surgeon, tried to explain to her that her feelings were largely hormonal, a result of chemicals released during pregnancy, labor, and delivery, and that eventually, rather quickly even, they would pass and she might think about the child wistfully from time to time but that she would not regret her decision. She argued, through her tears, that it had not exactly been her decision. Her father gave up and left the room. Her mother, a woman at this point in her life too vain and too horrified by the idea of becoming a grandmother to entertain the thought that her daughter might actually keep the baby, emphasized how much work it was to raise a child, and how much early adulthood of her own Anna had left ahead of her, too much to derail or squander on an infant. She herself had had an abortion before she had gotten married, she reminded Anna, and to this day she rarely thought about it. (This was not entirely accurate: her own parents had wasted no opportunity to make her feel terrible about the scandal, and every subsequent decision in her life had flowed from that experience of profound shame.) She had not made her own daughter feel ashamed about getting pregnant; on the contrary, she felt modern and compassionate for having accepted Anna's determined stance against having an abortion, although it could be surmised that this was in no small part because it was so late in the pregnancy when Anna had revealed the state of things. Now the sun was setting somewhere on the other side of the city, and the light was fading over the river. This was the time in American history when photographers were discovering new lenses and filters and retouching techniques that gave the glossy images in magazines a burnished, affluent glow. This was the glow that was spreading across the sky right now, a sheen that gave the river a metallic, artificial magic and glimmered bewitchingly on the buildings and highways. Anna's mother did not leave the room. She sat in the silence. She observed an orange triangle of light reflected from the window onto the blank television screen suspended from the ceiling. Had Anna turned on the television she might have heard about the death earlier that day of Count Basie, the celebrated bandleader whose music had captured the romance and optimism of another era. Or she might have caught a glimpse of a new form of entertainment called a music video, on a new channel known as MTV. But Anna did not turn on the television, and she did not respond to her mother. She was unmoved by her parents' arguments, unruly in her devotion to her infant daughter, and unhinged by the possibility that she might never hold her baby in her arms. She screamed. She screamed until the nurses and orderlies had to medicate away the screams. A doctor spoke to Anna's parents and wrote a prescription. Evidently there *were* antidepressants. They had not yet been perfected, however, and so Anna's screams continued long after her parents had brought her home. Finally, after two weeks of uninterrupted screams, it was arranged for the respectable and now ungrateful couple who had been waiting outside the delivery room to adopt a different baby. Their new baby was also American, not a Chinese or African baby. There really was no global village. It was 1984. When Anna finally had her beloved back in her arms, she gazed into her daughter's eyes for a long time. Then she looked up at her parents, whose own expressions were no longer able to conceal their disappointment and disgrace, shook the bangs from her eyes, and deadened her gaze somewhat before breaking into a smile. Then she said:

I'm going to name her Honor.

Anna's mother, in spite of herself, fell deeply in love with the child. She had imbued the drama of her only daughter's illegitimate pregnancy with all of the pathos and regret that she felt about her own marriage and divorce and therefore once the baby was born believed strongly that this child in possession of a single teenage mother must be in need of toys. She thought about her granddaughter all the time, took care of her while Anna finished high school, and was heartbroken when Anna took Honor with her to college. Her apartment was covered in pictures of the little girl. Most of these showed Honor staring into the camera, a profusion of curls dancing around her head, one hand reaching out to touch the lens. Her eyes were a startling, electric blue. Her nose a squat pug. Her neck thin like the stick of a lollipop. Her mouth curved in a mature amusement beyond her years. She had caused the ruination of one life, so her grandmother believed, and resuscitated another, and from this the woman deduced that the child was destined for calamity and splendor.

The afternoon was a cloudy haze. The branches of the trees in the park trembled like etchings come momentarily to life. The little girl, just walking, bent down and found a penny on the path that encircled the toy-boat pond.

It was a dirty copper specimen bent slightly at one edge and embossed upon it was the date 1923. What the little girl did on that cloudy day with the March wind tossing her curls into her face was to lift the penny to her lips, put it on her tongue, taste its cold filthy sweetness, and swallow it. Pigeons sailed overhead, their shadows skating on the pond, and in front of the little girl, out of the sleeve of a wool coat, a gloved hand emerged and pulled her toward home.

Over the years the little girl had moments of sudden restlessness when she would begin to feel the quickening motion of the globe as well as her own small self delicately balanced on the spinning ball. She sensed the rapid palpitations of her heart. She was aware of her blood pulsing through her limbs. She had reached an age when her young mother felt that she could leave her alone without worrying, and consequently Honor was deeply acquainted with solitude. She read early and often and was currently, at the age of eight, inhaling, if not actually comprehending, *Gone with the Wind* and the complete works of Agatha Christie. She felt that her tenuous circumstances—the two of them lived now in a college town while her mother was in graduate school, with only minimal support from Honor's grandparents, who were upset by Anna's refusal to return to New York—created an uncertain, wavering, and often wondrous atmosphere around their daily life which was not at all like the concrete, material world she read about in the newspapers, or even novels. The days seemed to float along without any tether to the organized rituals she observed at friends' houses: dinnertimes, bathtimes, bedtimes. In her house, time was a fluid, untamable vapor and anything, Honor felt, could happen.

It was in this spirit of anticipation that she would look out the window of their second-floor apartment waiting for her mother to return from a class or a cup of coffee with a friend, and would try to commit the street scene to memory in case she was called upon by the police to make a report in the event of her mother's disappearance. Her powers of concentration and observation were absurd. She accepted this burden as perfectly normal. She never questioned that it was necessary for her to exert such mental discipline, just as she never questioned why she lived with the expectation that one day her mother would not come home. She took note of the colors of the cars as they drove by and the order in which they drove past. She watched the rain fall and studied the patterns of the drops on the window, the rhythmic timing with which one lone raindrop would slide down from the top to the bottom, snaking through the freckled surface of the glass, giving the impression that the window itself, overcome with emotion, had begun to cry. She memorized the look of the leaves as they waved back and forth to one another from the trees, and she envied their casual relationships. She memorized the clothes on the people who occasionally walked past the little house on the quiet street. She remembered their postures of worry or calm and she thought she could read entire lifetimes into the slope of a shoulder or the back of a head. Her memory was mystifying because she didn't appear to be thinking or even exerting the slightest effort as she took in so acutely the world. If a hand had been waved in front of her face while she was looking she would have registered it, but her eyes would have acknowledged not a flicker of awareness.

The young girl sat in front of the window and fixed her gaze on an insect traversing the glass in such a way that it appeared to be climbing up the side of the house across the street. The insect flew away. A man was sitting on the roof of the house across the street. Honor did not recognize him. She saw that he was wearing a blue windbreaker and khaki pants. His face was turned to his left as if he were waiting for someone and gazing across the rooftops for their arrival. His legs dangled down. The building was three stories high. Honor had never seen anybody up there before and now she stared with amazement as the man, who appeared to be anywhere from fifty to seventy years old, turned his head to look in the opposite direction. The young girl opened her mouth to call out to her mother but her mother was not home. She continued to stare at the man who had stood up and had put his hands in his pockets. Then he took his hands from his pockets, stretched his arms above his head as if he were about to perform a salutation to the sun, and as he lifted his arms two enormous dove-colored wings unfurled on either side of him. The young girl opened her mouth to exclaim, even though her mother was not home, but this time there was no sound because her powers of speech had been eclipsed by fear. The man stood on the roof with his wings outstretched for some time. They were the size of American flags and their feathers looked thick and soft from a distance. They did not appear to be shadows or a mirage. The man was wearing sneakers. He folded back his wings, and the space around him returned to its usual emptiness.

There was no one walking down the quiet street. Honor, as if instructed by some higher self, left the house and called up to the man. He was friendly and unthreatening and he climbed down from the roof, wingless, and accepted her invitation inside. He was an angel. He was thinking of working in the neighborhood. He subverted her expectation of those in his profession with his plain, almost bland demeanor. He seemed sad. He was an average height, medium-build man, handsome in his youth obviously, with a healthy complexion and a muscular torso that moved gracefully within the confines of his blue windbreaker. He had a full head of graying hair that was ruffled from the wind and clear green eyes that took in everything. He was very polite to the little girl and asked her questions about herself. This struck her as appropriate. She answered him. Then they went into the kitchen and she poured iced tea from a pitcher in the refrigerator because it was the kind of thing that she had seen her mother do for guests. They sat down on the sofa in the living room and he drank his tea heartily. The room was neat and sparsely decorated mainly with bookshelves, in a typical graduate student style. The angel scanned the shelves. He noticed many books about music. In response to his question about them Honor explained that her mother was studying musicology. Did she have any instruments in the house, he wondered. Honor stood up and brought in a weathered black saxophone case. It was heavy for her and she swayed backwards as she carried it, relieved when she handed it to him. The angel relaxed and leaned back into the sofa. He opened the case. He smiled at the unpolished instrument. He stood up and began to play. He was not without talent. He closed his eyes. Honor listened to him and didn't bother about remembering the music. He spent a while playing something slow and swinging, like a sultry lullaby, for the little girl. When it was time for him to leave she saw him to the door. She shook his hand, because she had also seen her mother do that, but she wasn't really ready to say good-bye and so she followed behind him for a bit as he walked down the center of the empty street. Then she turned around and went back into the house in time to look out the window and see his blue shape diminishing into the distance. She put the saxophone away and waited for her mother to come home.

CHAPTER EIGHT

2005

Honor stood up in the subway car where she had been sitting and looked out into the darkness. Her stop was coming and she liked the moment before the light broke through the window. There was her reflection in the glass, a ghost with a shifting skeleton and a visible heartbeat as the columns and dim lights that made up the architecture of this underworld scrolled through her body rapid-fire in the blackness. Then she disappeared into the light. She turned toward the doors. She adjusted the strap of the bag slung across her chest and quickly stepped onto the platform.

It was raining softly when she emerged onto the street. She seemed to be looking through a scrim as she made her way along the sidewalk. From a distance, she appeared to be almost marching, silently, through the mist. With her steady gaze and long coat, her faded satchel and heavy

boots, she looked both present and ancient. She looked like
some beautiful soldier arrived from history.

You're here, she said.
   I'm here, he said.
   That's something, she said.
   It is.

They had called her and told her he was ready to see her
again. It had been several months. At night, she had
dreamt about him over and over. At night, she had read his
bones. Now back in the hospital she was afraid to look at
him, afraid to remind him that she knew him, afraid she
might lose him again. He didn't say much. He didn't talk
about what had happened. It went on this way for weeks,
as if nothing had ever happened between them. Then one
day when she came in he was sitting in his wheelchair, not
on the table. The nurse had gone.
   He said: So what do you think was going on with
that woman who lied her way into the photographer's
apartment?
   The one whose husband was court-martialed? The
pregnant one?
   She's not pregnant when she goes into the apartment.
   I know.
   So who is she? What does she want in there?
   She looked around the room. Can I take off my coat?
   No. He was smiling.
   Okay.

She sat on the table. She took off her bag and put it down next to her. She fiddled with a string she had tied around her wrist. She hadn't realized until now that she was nervous.

He stared at her, not fully believing that she was back. He blinked. He was bouncing his foot.

So, he said. The woman's pregnant, he said. Her husband's court-martialed, then a couple of years later, because that's what it seemed like to me, she basically breaks into this older woman's apartment. What's going on?

You got me.

He looked down. She could sense his expression change without seeing his face. She saw it in the line of his shoulders, the top of his head.

I tried to hurt myself while you were gone, he said.

They told me, she said. I'm glad you're okay. I'm glad you're still here.

Then he looked back up.

Don't leave again.

I didn't leave. You wouldn't see me.

You can't listen to me. You can't listen to them. If I say that again, don't listen.

What should I do?

Find me. Come here anyway.

All right. I will.

He looked at her like he knew she was going to save him.

Then he said: So what happens next?

She shrugged her shoulders. Her hair lifted up and down.

Only one way to find out.

1936

Joe was driving along a curving parkway, heading north. A white sign with green lettering said Entering Massachusetts. Vivian sat next to him reading from a piece of paper covered with a scrawl of directions. It began to rain. Light steady rain dotted the air in quick flashes, hyphenating the atmosphere, making dashes of white against the dark brown trees. November, and a silver sky was throwing out this water, indifferent to the cars, the lives, the minor tragedies and great loves below, an oblivious sky. Vivian thought they might be lost but Joe said how could they be they were supposed to be in Massachusetts and here they were. He looked over at her and smiled and the furrow in her brow melted but still she had been short with him. She had not promised anything. The trip had been his idea and she had agreed to go but she had not promised it would be easy. She went back to studying the piece of paper. She exuded always a sense that they were in the wrong. He could feel it in her hesitation. She waited a moment before answering him. She picked up one topic, then put it down before it went too far and chose another. She put her hand on his arm and then took it away, as if he were a sculpture in a museum that she had momentarily been driven to touch. He was flattered that she tried at all, that she was here at all, and he respected her wary conscience. It relieved him of the need to have much of one himself. It made it possible for him to put his energy toward persuading her and reassuring her and comforting her.

But he was also aware that this was wrong. It was just that he could not possibly stop himself. His being in this car with Vivian was as inevitable as this silver rain that kept falling. He loved her and they were having an adventure that felt as new as the trees wet and slick with fresh cold rain. Their time together felt as sad as it was exciting but it would never have made any sense to him to think that this feeling was simply him, that it was the feeling that he had been carrying around for many years and now with her it had found its perfect expression. It was not in his repertoire of ideas to consider that his feelings were not a result of what was going on around him but that his feelings actually existed somewhere inside. He was not fortunate or unfortunate enough to know that he was the source of the feeling. That was something he could not possibly have known.

When they found their way to a part of Quincy, Massachusetts, called Norfolk Downs to see the factory of the world's greatest cymbal maker, the rain disappeared and the sky surged with blue and the air turned their faces bright and red and their eyes were clear.

2005

They put Milo in a different room. They had thought he was getting better and then when it had become clear that although his legs were improving his mind was not, they had kept him under closer observation. He was not allowed anything that could be used as rope. They kept his clothes in a separate place. He had tied several T-shirts

together and when they'd asked him about it he had said
he was making a scarf. For a while he had wanted to forget
her and he tried but then the stories kept coming back
even when she wasn't there. Not new stories, just the same
images haunting him and pulling him back into wondering, wanting to know. When he'd said he needed to see her
again and they'd asked him why he'd said: Because I want
to know what happens. They had no idea what he meant
but they'd taken it as a good sign.

They had let him keep the same bed, although the
sheets were different. Just a kind of sleeping bag that he
couldn't twist into anything. He didn't want to anyway.

He wanted to unravel the story instead. What did the
story of the photographer have to do with Joe? Who was
the pregnant woman? At first Joe had seemed like a fraud
to him, some wannabe artist dreaming of romance. And
Vivian too, what a poseur. With her airs and so aloof. Pearl
had seemed like the only real one, the only sympathetic
figure. And here they were, taking this long-suffering
woman for granted, ruining her life. But then he'd begun
to realize what Pearl and Joe had been through and he felt
sorry for them both, not just her. He could see how Joe
might need some escape. He was a kind of idiot, Milo
thought, but an understandable idiot. Someone he could
recognize and if not forgive then at least accept. And
Vivian, he began to see her too as more confused than
aloof, more defensive than pretentious. And she really did
care about music and art more than just about anything.
He was starting to believe that. And now here she had a
chance for some love. He didn't know why she had never
had any before but he knew this to be true. He could see
them all from a great distance as though they were jewels

in his hand, crystals that split the light into different colors and directions depending on which way they fell in his palm, where they landed, the time it took for light to land on them. He held them in his hand like tears that had spilled there and turned to gems and he watched their facets shift and their hues change and he felt no judgment and no anger toward them and no sorrow for them either. Only a pity that was more like interest, a deep concern. He wanted to know what would happen to them. He wanted to know who they really were.

Of course who could they possibly be if not some part of him, Milo Hatch, a wounded soldier living in a VA hospital? But he could not think of any way in which they were connected to him. His family had lived for generations in Maine, and their history had its own, utterly different, story. No, this story had nothing literally to do with him. It must have something to tell him, but it was not his story.

So, Joe wasn't a fraud exactly and Honor hadn't disappeared. Those mysteries were solved. But what about the woman breaking into the apartment? Milo thought about her and her story. She had been shaken by the verdict, her husband's dismissal from the army. Would it ruin his career? Would the trauma hurt her pregnancy? And what did the photographer have to do with any of this? He couldn't think of any clues other than the wedding photograph of Pearl and Joe. But that didn't tell him much. His only hope was Honor.

He thought of her and the gems in his palm melted back into tears and the tears went flying up to his eyes and moved through him and settled back into his chest and returned to being what they had originally been, those burning embers. He hated that he couldn't figure this out alone. He hated that the story wouldn't move forward without Honor. Then he realized that this feeling toward her was like Joe's feeling toward Vivian, that he needed her, or Joe's feeling for Pearl, that she was somehow in his way. Milo recognized that neither view was fair to Honor. She was a person. She was trying to help. Then he saw her too from a distance and she was a jewel in his hand. She was like a jewel in a story that when placed in the proper location would unlock the treasure chest, the trapdoor, the secret wall. The story could not go on without her. He could not go on without her. And the light moved through her and she was strange to him, and radiant.

Honor

As it happened the man in the blue windbreaker never returned to Honor's street. There was no sign that her existence would be anything but ordinary. She grew up. As the years passed and the time to earn her own living approached, she waited for a sign that she might have a calling. She knew that she possessed an uncommon discipline of mind and a fierce sensitivity to the physical world but she did not know what to do with these endowments. She was a slender girl with a strong body and a desire to express herself through movement, but she appreciated the difficulty of economic survival and was aware that she might not be able to make money by becoming a dancer, which was her dream. Her interest in reading had not declined, but she had seen how little books had to do with her strange world and she felt too vibrantly alive for their dry pages. In the meantime, her mother drifted from low-paying employment to low-paying employment. Creditors would have to be assuaged, arrangements were always pending, logistics seemed to consume her existence. Anna lifted the papers on her desk and rearranged them. The headstrong young girl who had bravely taken on the challenge of motherhood had, in spite of her wish to take care of her daughter, grown up into a confused and distracted woman. Neither mother nor daughter was unmindful of the dangers that they chronically encountered through the annoying encroachment of real life and its responsibilities and demands. Yet they were united in their bafflement as to how to respond to them. Their little family unit seemed to thrive in a state of extended crisis. But one day Honor knocked a spoon off the table at dinner and when she bent down to pick it up she caught sight of her concave reflection in the oval of tarnished silver and saw that she was no longer a little girl. When she emerged in the upright position she had decided to change her personality. She would be courageous and independent as befitted a young woman at the beginning of the twenty-first century. Anna stood up to get something and, having forgotten what it was, sat down again. Honor looked at her mother across the table and a hitherto undiscovered reservoir of compassion rocked like an ocean in her chest. She swayed slightly from the waves of feeling. The next day she left home and found work as a dancer.

1936

The factory was located on Fayette Street. It appeared to Joe to be nothing more than a series of sheds and was in fact formerly a garage. It had been chosen by Aram because of its proximity to the ocean, for tempering cymbals in sea water, and resembled his centuries-old factory in Istanbul as closely as possible. Aram had come from Turkey to teach his nephew the art of making cymbals. It was the family profession and required the use of a secret formula that Aram had come to impart in person. He was an upright gentleman with an old-country demeanor. He could be found sitting out in front of the factory and striking gleaming metal discs with his felt-covered hammer. The chimes could be heard high above the noises of the alley.

They made the cymbals the way they had always been made, the way Aram's ancestors had made them in Turkey. There was a secret unwritten formula that only the family knew. A copper alloy was mixed and shaped into a molten pancake and fired until it glowed orange in the depths of a gigantic furnace. The cymbal makers did this again and again until the metal hardened into a thin black disk. Then they stamped the center of the cup by machine and returned it to the oven yet again to add a sweet lightness, Aram told them, to the tone of the cymbal. After this the inchoate instrument was hammered for hours by hand and then left to season. For two weeks it went untouched. Then it was tested every other day over the course of two more weeks until it was deemed ready. Each shining cymbal required one month of labor to be born.

When Vivian and Joe pulled up, Aram greeted Vivian with a smile. He welcomed them inside. She had met him in one of the clubs in Harlem where he had gone to meet with drummers to learn their language and find out how to make better cymbals for them. Vivian had known some drummers back then, she explained quietly. Aram invited them in and made tea. Vivian's eyes shone with a curiosity and excitement Joe had rarely seen. Then Aram began to tell stories about Gene Krupa and Jo Jones and Chick Webb and Joe listened with his hat in his hand. Aram talked about how Gene wanted his cymbals to be thinner and thinner. He talked about the Hi-Hat, or sock cymbal, and how it had helped change the character of American music because it had changed the way drummers kept time—before the Hi-Hat most drummers used press rolls on the snare drum or cowbells, woodblocks, and other percussion to keep time. When they began keeping time with the cymbals, that was the beginning of swing.

Later, in the car, Joe said: I feel like with you I can do that, keep time. I feel like with you it is always now.

But you can't keep time, Joe. Not really.

He turned the car quickly, hand over hand.

I guess that's why I like swing.

But you're not even a drummer, Joe. You play the saxophone.

I guess I'd always dreamt of being a drummer. But it doesn't matter. It's the music. The cymbals moving the music forward. I love that sound. You do too.

She was looking out the window. The rain had come back.

I'll leave her, he said. I have to. We've tried to make each other happy but we don't.

She turned back to look at him. I can't promise I'll make you happy either.

You already have, he said. That won't change.

There you go again, she said, thinking that you can keep time.

They found a new way to keep time, he said. Let me try.

Honor wasn't the kind to leave. She'd never left anyone, except Anna, and that was different because in her own way Anna had already left her many years before. But this was what she could not tell Milo, that people seemed to leave her, that one day there had been a phone call. They weren't married or even engaged and so it wasn't an official phone call. It was from his family, who'd found her number among his things. They'd met her twice. He was the one who had given her the book of Ralph Ellison essays. He was the one who had taught her about music. She had been walking down the street and it was the middle of the day and there was a howling all around her from traffic, trucks, the population steadily screaming through the city under siege as it was every day. The cell phone was pressed against her wet cheek and the cars screeched past and Honor was trying to wipe away tears with the back of her hand and a stranger caught her eye and looked at her with a momentary and truthful look of pity and compassion and she knew that everyone, everyone, everyone would always leave her.

CHAPTER NINE

1969

When she stood up to leave the restaurant the murals on the wall tilted and it looked like the Venetian gondolas were sailing straight to hell. The head curator held his liquor better and the benefactors seemed perfectly normal but the photographer rarely drank and so now she was wobbling and a centrifugal force spun around in her head. They walked her to the corner. The curator was saying something about the press for the show and doing interviews and had she been in *Vogue* before and she was trying to walk slowly but kept falling behind and she saw the very fashionable women in midtown wearing what would be the beginnings of the Seventies look, wide pants, wide collars, but for now most of the ladies were still demure as if the Sixties had not really happened here on Fifth Avenue. Even she, a painter, could have stepped more from the late Fifties with her pocketbook and headband but when she got home she would throw on her jeans. Oh to be home. To get away from the heavy leather menus and banquettes of midtown and back to her contemplative mess, her wavy glass windows, her cameras and slides. They didn't wait long with her at the corner. The ladies sailed into cabs and the curator turned around and headed back to the museum. She was alone again and when the bus came she felt small and clear and free.

Walking up the stairs to her apartment she sensed the head-spinning return and wished she knew about those hangover remedies her alcoholic artist friends were always fixing for themselves on mornings at beach houses or in the afternoon when she might come over to their studios. But she did not know of any and had no desire to call anyone. The pathetic let-down feeling after a business lunch left her wanting only to work. That was all that would repair her, and perhaps that alone would wipe away the drink.

She turned the key in the lock and opened the door.

The mantel and the water glass left on the mantel were still there but there was a difference in the room and she glanced around before stepping inside. There was the door to the little bedroom slightly more ajar than she would have left it. There was a different position of the bags stacked under the long table, an almost undetectable shift in the shape the bags made in relation to one another and she stood for a moment wondering if this was just the alcohol or if the light had changed so much that objects seemed to have moved and then she scanned the top of one of her desks and she saw that it was empty. This was when she rushed into the apartment and touched the top of the desk to see if she was imagining this emptiness and then spread her arms out over the desk and then laid her head down on the desk and made a low moaning sound into the tabletop as if it were a body she was crying into.

She spent the rest of the day and night looking all over the apartment for her film and slides but they were gone. These were the photographs that were going to be in the exhibition. These were photographs for her first show of color work. These were photographs she had taken over the last five years, mainly of children, children she had found and watched on the streets. She loved the children in the photographs and she loved the photographs. In the photographs she had captured the weird shapes and beautiful shadows and the anger and calm and sweet openness of the children. She had taken pictures of life. It was the only life she cared about anymore. Now it was gone. Now, she was gone.

The photographer sat for a long time looking out the big window into the quiet, darkening garden. Her apartment faced a distant brick wall. She watched the shadows on the wall and thought about the shadows in her life and in her pictures. She wondered how this had happened and why. She cried and in the morning after thinking for a long time about who might have done this, she made a decision. Then she called the police.

2005

Do you think she ever gets the pictures back?

I think so. I think she will. She seems to have some idea about who took them.

Honor could hear in her own voice that she wanted to believe what she was saying. Her words sounded transparent, like footsteps on a bridge.

What makes you say that? said Milo. I don't think she has any idea. I don't know if she'll get them back. Unless maybe the police get a description of the woman from that old lady downstairs.

I hope so. It's so sad if she never gets them back.

She was hearing the footsteps in her voice walk away.

Milo craned his neck around and then pushed himself up onto his elbow. Why are you crying?

I'm not sure.

He took a corner of the sheet that had been draped over him and wiped her tears.

Thanks, she said.

Then the sheet slipped away and he was wiping her tears with his hands. Then she was sitting beside him, and he was holding her while she cried.

I'm sorry, she said, lifting her head from his shoulder. I don't know why this is making me so sad.

Don't be sorry, he said. It's okay.

She looked at him and her eyes were wet and shining and the lids were reddened and her long lashes fanned around them like feathers around an egg. She had the unusually present look of a figure in a painting, someone to whom a great message is about to be revealed. She looked like she was about to receive something.

I think I need to know who stole those pictures, she said. I can't explain why, but I feel like it matters to me in some way that is impossible to explain.

Now the footsteps were gone entirely. Not even an echo. She was saying what she meant.

All right. We'll find out. He was stroking her hair.

Milo, I'm sorry, this isn't supposed to be about me.

It isn't supposed to be anything. It's just a story.

She laughed a little. You're right. So why do I care?

You care because you're a caring person.

That's when she put her hand on his neck and it brushed his collarbone and he flinched and pulled away. There was a look on his face that pierced her.

I'm so sorry, she said. Let's forget about this.

I can't forget about it, he said.

Then he took her hand and put it back on the same part of his collarbone and a flash burst in her brain as if she herself were made of light and she saw the reflection of a woman's hand curved and distorted in the brass of a saxophone and then a shimmering sound swept through her and she was dancing in a crowded room.

She pulled her hand off. It's too much, she said.

What about here, he said. He put her hand on his shoulder and she saw the perspiration blooming on the back of the woman's dress in the courtroom in New Orleans. She saw the man standing in uniform with his back to her. She felt the woman tremble when the verdict was called out.

And here, he said. He put her hand on his back and she saw Pearl warming coffee on the stove and the odd lavender light that came at sunset into the little apartment coloring the white stove and the yellowing cabinets and the stained porcelain sink.

Here, he said, and now her hand was lower on his back and she saw Joe and Vivian in Greenwich Village, sitting by the river, driving to Massachusetts, talking in a car with the rain hitting the windows.

Then he moved her hand to his neck and she saw a

woman swaying underwater, her black hair floating weightlessly like ink. Then the woman became one of many women, hundreds of bodies swaying like underwater tombstones.

I can't do this, she said.

She closed her eyes.

Why not? he said.

She opened her eyes and looked at him. Then she looked down.

I can't do this to you. It's too much.

He dipped his head as if to look into her downcast eyes. He smiled. He lifted his chin as though he could lift her up with a simple gesture.

I can take it, he said. He was still smiling. I've taken worse. He whispered: We'll figure it out.

She allowed herself to look at him.

Don't you see? he said. It's all inside me.

She was scared now and he was the one who seemed unafraid.

I'm the one who can help you now, he said.

So I wasn't even able to do my job. She looked away again, her eyes tearing.

No, this is your job. This isn't pitying me. This is giving me some way to fight for you. This is what I do best.

His face was lit up and there wasn't the usual anger around his mouth. He looked younger and older at the same time.

She wiped her eyes and gave him a pained smile that he thought was inhumanly pretty.

Always a soldier, Honor said.

Your soldier, he said.

CHAPTER TEN

Vivian

She saw him at night in her dreams a dark figure
shadowing her along a riverbank and catching up
with her the boats in the river sliding past ghostly
passengers watching her in her final moments on shore
because he was coming for her that much was certain and
he would bring her back with him and he was coming
closer she could feel him he was a mystery in the blackness
that she kept trying to deny but their reflections in the
dark water were even darker and as his approached hers
there was the reflection of the saxophone case too like some
mad sea animal searching for her, hunting her down and
now they were right beside her and she would have to give
over to this wrong love or she would lose him or she could
fall over into the water and it would all be over she would
just let herself fall into the river and then she was falling
and the water grabbed her hungrily and she sped down a
dark channel and in the dark water weeds and debris

wound around her as she was pulled quickly by the current and then it stopped the dream stopped and she woke up screaming and he wasn't there how could he be he was not supposed to be she had told him to go home he was supposed to be home she was not his home.

She had not wanted to go with Pearl to meet him at the dock. She had not found Pearl interesting and so assumed he would not interest her either. He had wiped his palm on his shirt. He had seemed ordinary. But then the way he had looked at her in the kitchen had moved something inside her and she had felt seen although she had hidden that from him. She was still very young. Younger than either Pearl or Joe and they had struck her at first as old and sad and only later as experienced. She had traveled. She had been educated. But they had experience. They had sorrow. Maybe it was his sorrow that was looking at her in the kitchen and found hers. A sorrow that lifted when it felt his and soared like a note of music soars. A note of music soars, she thought, because it is trying to find its way back.

She would forget him. Vivian had decided that for the first time on the way home from Joe and Pearl's apartment. She had a dying father to care for, a distraught mother, a life to begin. She had friends from college, mostly rich girls, not scholarship girls like herself, girls whose families didn't seem to know there was a Depression, girls who invited her to parties, girls who didn't know about the latest music and who used her to find out about things that seemed slightly dangerous. She had those friends but she was false with them because they could not understand her life and because she could never have told them about Joe. Years later, when their husbands had died and they had started careers of their own and raised many children and found new husbands or not, years later they would have been sympathetic to her stories about Joe. But for now she avoided most of the girls she knew from school.

Once she had met him again in the pastry shop she avoided almost everything but him. His fingers around the handle of his saxophone case, his long legs on the cobblestone streets, his soulful playing, the way he looked to her for a wisdom which somehow she had but had never really wanted, his voice that had a deep mellow comfort in it, these were the things she did not avoid now. This was the tender misery that she did not avoid now.

We have to say good-bye, she said. This really isn't possible.

I know, he said. But then he whispered: Let's just keep saying good-bye.

The woman in the education department of the Brooklyn Children's Museum looked more closely at her outfit than at her résumé. Vivian could tell that the woman approved of her shoes. You can start on Monday, she said. Vivian liked tying the smocks around the children's wriggling waists, handing the big brushes into their tiny starfish hands. She sponged tables. She set out paints. She truly appreciated the work they made and hung it up on the walls of the room. Still, the streets at the end of the day stretched on and she imagined that around a corner she might find a glorious church or a wide-open piazza like the places she had visited in Europe. The sound of a wailing instrument played in her head. I am too young to feel this lonely, she thought.

She met him at night at the movies. The curtains were dark red. On the balcony ornate carvings swirled and twisted as if they were alive. The ushers smoked and bent their heads in the lobby while the movie scrolled along and the faces up on the screen were as gigantic as gods come down to earth to impart their complete and utter lack of understanding. They had no answers. They fought and cried. Their enormous velvety eyes and their white marble teeth looked at nothing real and said nothing real and yet their flickering presence made her press more closely into his arms and the feeling in those arms made her less afraid than she had ever been. She thought: This is love. I can't really have it, but at least I know now what it is.

And then he said that they could be together. He said they would be. She said that he was trying to hold on to something that couldn't be held, to keep time. He said: Let me try.

She woke up in the middle of the night and this time he was there. They were in Massachusetts, at an inn. All was quiet except the wind outside, which she realized she could hardly hear above the beating in his chest where she had rested her head.

In the morning he was still there, which amazed her. They drove to a pretty town where the houses were white clapboard with black shutters and some bright red and orange leaves were still left on some of the trees and the November sky turned uncharacteristically blue and people said hello. She could imagine living in a place like this. Her hand fit into his. Wind blew down the pretty streets as if they were continually being washed of any dirt or dust or anything unwanted. Air swept up into the high branches and made a soft strong blowing sound. She thought of horns. She told him and he squeezed her hand. They ate at a tiny restaurant for lunch and there were buoys on the walls and netting and they ate fish. The sea came inside here. She could feel the salt on her face. She thought it would be nice to be with Joe in the summertime at the sea. She saw his hair standing sideways and a dark blue ocean lifting up behind him. They had wine. He toasted the two of them. She saw his mouth through her wineglass while he spoke. She was used to seeing her life through a pane of glass but now when he put down his drink and she put down hers she saw things clearly with nothing between her and her life and smiled and he said, You know I'm not sure I've ever really seen you smile before and I can tell you that nothing has ever looked so beautiful. I'm going to make you do that again.

Back at the inn it was their last day together like this for who knew how long and every moment felt like a last moment and they enjoyed it but she said she would not give herself to him completely until he had told Pearl. It wasn't right. And he looked in her green eyes and he knew that she meant it and so he did not try to change her mind.

There were sock cymbals and Low Boys and Hi-Hats for keeping time. There were larger cymbals for punctuation, riding, and choking. There were cymbals with names like Plop, Sizzle, Sting, Whang, and Swish. And there were the very thinnest cymbals of all. Cymbals with a sharp brilliant tone that could instantly be damped, cymbals with a silver resonance. It was the shimmering sound of cymbals that she would later think had made them fall in love. A silver sound that led the music and kept time and moved life forward. A sound of fantasy and romance that swept up the whole world. A sound that was made in America. It came by way of Istanbul but most people didn't know that. It was a sound that people thought was the essence of America: light and swinging and free. But it was a sound that had explosions in it. "Our business is hazardous," Avedis said. Even with his experience he was apt to have an explosion once a week. In the beginning, the factory had so many explosions that their insurance company canceled the policy and returned the premiums paid in advance. When he told Joe, Joe said, Too bad you can't get insurance for everyday life. I could really use some of that.

At night, again, the beating of his heart under her head. She woke him up. What will she do without you? she said. He was half asleep, in love, not thinking, mostly dreaming. He said: She'll probably be better off.

.

She couldn't sleep. She pulled a chair up to the window and looked out at the sleeping town. Across the street, one of those perfect white clapboard houses. She looked at the shape of the house and the relationship of the windows to one another and the moonlight bathing the house in a calm but tragic yellow and blue light. She thought for the first time in a long time about painting that light. She went back to bed and instead of putting her head on his chest, she held his hand.

CHAPTER ELEVEN

Milo and Honor

Milo saw a white clapboard house on the ceiling. A raw damp smell of ocean air flew through the room. Suddenly lights arrived in the windows of the floating house and out came big-band music as if heard from a distant radio, Count Basie playing from Kansas City. When he opened his eyes Honor was holding his hand.

You were saying something to me, calling me.
     There was a house on the ceiling and it was swinging.
     I see, she said.
     Then: What was I saying?
     Something about the Bosphorus, a tipping boat, a pavilion carved out of jewels. I've just been sitting here holding your hand. Then you pulled away and I put my hand on

your arm. That's when you started talking. When I touched your arm the story changed.

He was back now, sitting up. He shook the hair from his eyes. His face had been filling out again. He looked healthier, stronger.

There was something about cymbals coming from Turkey, wasn't there? The beginning of everything, the origin of all this music and mess. If we understand how all of this got started, even if it's just a myth, a story that isn't true, maybe we can make some sense out of what went on with Vivian and Joe, what's going on with us. That older guy from Constantinople, the cymbal maker, was I talking about him?

I don't think so. It seemed like you were talking about a woman, a girl really. It seemed like you were the girl, talking through her.

Where was it that you put your hand?

She pointed to a spot on his arm below his shoulder where the muscle twisted, and he grabbed her wrist.

Keep it there, he said.

1623

In the orchard, on her way to the New Palace, the girl tried to jump out of the carriage, but the eunuch stopped her with his hand on her arm. It was a touch that did not so much hurt her as communicate a desire to keep her alive.

Later, she had a bruise, which the Sultan found charming. Turning back to sit solemnly in the midst of four

escorts, she found herself frightened by the sight of sunlight licking the small tough leaves on the fruit trees. She
didn't know what to expect—the stories of what lay ahead
for her were so strange they seemed impossible to
believe—but she knew that without the force of that hand
on her arm her fear would have made her run straight to
her death.

They had bathed her and rubbed rose oil on her body
before swathing her in layers of colored silk. Her veil
panted above her mouth. She could smell the sea. At one
point on the ride they crossed a garden and looking out of
the carriage she saw hundreds of flowers, vivid yellows
and pinks and reds that smeared across her vision and
made her want to vomit. The carriage itself was festooned
with roses and tulips and carnations. The perfume was
overpowering, poisonous. The carriage stopped at the
Gate of Felicity.

Flanked by two escorts on either side, she entered the
Third Court. She was not taken to the White Eunuchs'
Quarters or to the Throne Room or to the Library, but
instead accompanied directly to the Royal Chamber. In her
confusion, she thought the grapes depicted in the shimmering mosaic that confronted her when she entered were
real, and she sensed her mouth watering, instinctively. The
luxury and almost disgusting beauty of the room were
familiar to her from having seen the Valide Sultan's suite,
but what she witnessed here was of another magnitude. It
was a terrifying sumptuousness, and she felt an ache of
pleasure in the midst of her fear. When the eunuchs left
her, she tried to meet the eyes of the one who had stopped
her from jumping, but he held his gaze steadily in front of

him, his lips firmly set, his long black lashes only slightly darker than his skin, and seemed as unreachable as the grapes in the mosaic.

She was waiting, for many hours, on heaps of pillows and embroidered sheets. Women had come to attend to her, but she had not been fed, and as her hunger and anxiety escalated, she passed her hands nervously over the fabrics surrounding her, and felt every gold thread like a needle in her skin. An old woman named Kaya was mainly responsible for her, and had brought her water. In a moment of desperation she had blurted out, "My name is Parvin." "Farvin," Kaya repeated, because she had no front teeth.

She was waiting to be raped. She knew it and Kaya knew it. But it was not called rape and it was not thought of that way. It would have been considered treasonous, or demented, to have such a thought.

In her state of increasing panic, she imagined hundreds of birds were screeching and trying to enter the room through the space under the door. But as the sound grew more distinct she realized that it was the sound of swords scraping in their sheaths. She thought it must be the Sultan. The door opened, and in walked two of the eunuchs and a third man. They introduced him as the Royal Alchemist. He was a tall man, not Turkish but Armenian, and he had a mustache and long, compassionate eyebrows. He came toward her, slowly, and he could tell by her voice that she was Persian. She was talking now, feverishly, asking him to help her escape. His face was so gentle that she assumed he could rescue her. Which direction should I run? she asked, and he said, There are guards everywhere.

Hide me, then, she said, and his eyebrows angled more steeply, giving her hope. She was not aware, in her delirium, that he was as much a servant as she, and that although he would have loved to lift her up and run off with her in a cloud of colored silk, he had a job to perform. He was here to work.

He knelt down to look into her face and took her hand, almost as if he were a physician taking her pulse. He explained that he was a metalsmith, and that in addition to his practice of alchemy, he was a craftsman, that he made objects, including musical instruments.

"I understand you are a wonderful dancer," he said.

"Oh, no, not at all," she said. "I'm clumsy, and my arms are too long."

He told her that the Sultan had asked for her because he had seen her dance. He had seen her in his mother's, the Valide Sultan's, suite, where Parvin had been selected as a favorite and often performed for the head of the harem's entertainment. One of the girls would recite poetry and Parvin would move, using traditional steps but often inventing gestures of her own, and it was during one of these graceful exercises that the Sultan had spotted her through a curtain. He came often, to pay tribute to his mother and to enjoy the company of his consorts, but the time he had witnessed her dancing she had not been aware of his presence.

"The Sultan has requested that I make a special set of cymbals to be played while you perform for him. I am here to watch you dance, so that I can be inspired to create the perfect instruments."

She said that she usually performed to poetry, and that

in any case she was not moved at the moment to dance. Her delirium had transmuted into fearlessness, and now she said whatever she felt.

Then one of the two eunuchs stepped forward. He had been standing in the shadows and she hadn't realized until now that he was the one who had stopped her from jumping. He stepped forward and began to recite a passage from the great poet Firdusi. His shoulders were very broad and as he spoke his white tunic swelled with the energy from his lungs and chest. He looked straight ahead, and still would not meet her eyes, but his gaze was less stern now than before. For a moment, she thought she could sense him shaking slightly, but his words betrayed nothing; they were strong and clear and mellow. The quality of his voice reminded her of the wind pushing little waves far out on the ocean. For the first time in days she felt a lightness in her body. She stood up from the pillows and began to dance.

2005

Some nights after she left Milo, Honor would turn up the music until it thundered in her ears. She hoped that she would blow out an eardrum. She liked the crash of the cymbals in her head. The music was the music Sam had left her. Sam had played drums as a kid. He loved the sound of cymbals. Listen to them, he would say to her, they can shimmer or they can crack. Now, either way, they broke her heart. He'd taught her about how, in his humble opinion—he would say that, his humble opinion, ironically of course because he knew that there was nothing humble about him—he had taught her that so much of jazz was all about cymbals. Symbols? Like symbols on a sign or in a poem, she had asked, looking out the car window, because she hadn't really been paying attention. That's cute, he'd said. No, cymbals with a *c,* he went on, they really changed the music in this country because it was when they started using the cymbals for the beat that jazz really began to swing. Swing music, he said, it really all started with cymbals.

And where did cymbals start? she asked playfully, only somewhat curious. A pathetic attempt at flirting, she thought. She was unable to distract him.

That's a good question, he said thoughtfully. Always the teacher, always the journalist. Always honest:

I have no idea.

The Cymbal Maker

Avedis had a workshop far from the Sultan's chambers, on the other side of the palace grounds. Here he and his assistants made cups to be used in the baths, kitchens, and harems of the palace, and poured bronze for the enormous vessels in which the cooks prepared feasts for the Sultan. He was a metalsmith because his father, who had immigrated to Constantinople in 1598, had been a metalsmith. Avedis had done well in the family trade. Recently, he had been given authorization to make cymbals and bells for the Sultan's court. But his passion, his intellectual lust, was for alchemy. The Sultan, Murad IV, was indulgent of Avedis's interest not only because it promised riches, but because he had a taste for gold jewelry. A savage warrior who had had seventeen of his eighteen brothers murdered when he ascended to the throne, Murad evidently also saved a place in his heart for beauty. He was a drunk who loved the poets. He adored women and soulful music. And he dreamt of marrying his passions, as he had explained to Avedis while posing for a miniature portrait in jeweled chain mail armor, in a vision of Parvin, the Persian girl with the long limbs, dancing to the rhythm of heavenly cymbals. He wanted Avedis to create the perfect accompaniment to her movement, a sound that would capture her grace.

After seeing her dance himself, Avedis understood his Sovereign's obsession. His insides bled a little when he thought of her. Sitting in his workshop, hunched over a stained and ancient copy of Paracelsus' *The Tincture of the Philosophers,* he could not keep himself from picturing the curve of her elbow as it swept before her face, and the bend of her knee, seen behind folds of silk, as it dipped and allowed her ankles to soften and then push her delicate feet off the ground. He tried to concentrate on the words in front of him, which were explaining that all that was necessary to obtain the Philosopher's Stone was to mix and coagulate the "rose-colored blood of the Lion" and the "gluten of the Eagle," but it was hopeless. He heard over and over her pleas to him to help her escape, and he was ashamed at himself for having paid so little attention. But what could he have done? Risk execution for the sake of a girl he didn't know? He had worked long and hard to acquire his status within the palace, and his dream was to start his own factory in Constantinople. Besides, when she'd asked him, he hadn't yet seen her dance.

As soon as that thought bubbled in his brain, the rationalization disgusted him. He was a gentle man, but severe with himself. He seemed to seek out the same kind of magical perfection in his own behavior that he sought in his laboratory. But it was too late for nobility in action. Now he was left to wonder about her. What made her so headstrong and unhappy? Most of the girls in the harem would have been pleased to be picked by the Sultan. It was an opportunity to better their circumstances, perhaps even give birth to a princess and be taken care of for life, or to a prince and possibly become the Valide Sultan, the head of the harem and the true power behind the throne. Or, if the Sultan fell deeply for a consort, he might make her a Haseki, one of his favorites, and she could live in the New Palace, and receive a higher allowance than his own daughters. To be a Haseki was in many ways the most powerful position of all, and most girls in the harem would not even dream of such good fortune. But obviously the Sultan's latest infatuation had no craving for power or security. She appeared to live through her feelings alone: fear, need, dancing, abandon. Maybe she was too young to appreciate her situation; she looked to him to be about sixteen, although something in her eyes told him she was older. Or maybe she was just a fool. It didn't matter. His heart bent like one of his molten metals when he pictured her. He would have turned her to gold to save her, if he'd known how, but in spite of his years of study and experimentation, he did not. All he could hope to give her at this point was a set of cymbals that would do justice to her art, an instrument whose purity might equal hers, and, if he was lucky, whose vibrations might also contain a hint of the longing he felt for her—his, and this was how he had already begun to think of her, as *his*—his lovely and unobtainable, his mysterious and imprisoned Parvin.

CHAPTER TWELVE

1936

When will you tell her?

She already knows, Joe said.

How can you tell?

She suggested we go to see Basie, at Roseland. It wasn't like her. She doesn't like the music that much, and it's too expensive. She never thinks of that kind of thing.

She loves you very much.

She used to. Not anymore.

People don't really stop loving other people, Vivian said.

She had her head on his shoulder. Her hair in twisted ribbons down his back.

She's frightened, she said.

I'm frightened, he said.

He touched her face with his hand.

But you'll never stop loving me? he said.

I don't see how that's possible.

1623

In the mornings when she awoke, the Sultan was already gone. He left the bed sequined with silver coins, a sign that he was pleased, and every morning she collected the coins and threw them in the base of the ceramic pot where a leafy flowering plant grew in the corner. One day, as she was covering the coins with dirt, Kaya walked in wearing a tense expression on her face, and behind her was the eunuch. He nodded his head for Kaya to leave, which she did, but not before going over to the flowerpot and pretending to clean it, while quickly hiding the last of the coins. When she left and Parvin was alone with the eunuch, they stood facing each other for several long seconds before he spoke.

It was unexpected that there would be so much tension; the black eunuchs were in charge of the harem women and Parvin had spent almost her entire life in the harem. She had been followed by, tended to, practically siblings with these men. They had seen her unveiled, unclothed, unwashed. But she had never seen this man before the day he had stopped her from jumping out of the carriage, and she felt a deep and inevitable bond to him. She did not blame him for taking her to the Sultan because he had saved her life and he had done so even though—and this was absolutely clear to her—he had done it even though he had no illusions that her life included any more joy or hope or liberty than his. It was simply hers. He recognized that, and she wanted to thank him for it.

But before she could speak he explained to her that he had come to escort her to the northern end of the pleasure grounds between the Topkapi Saray and the seawalls along the Golden Horn. It was here that the Sultan liked to take his recreation, and he had planned an elaborate festivity that would last for several days. Members of the harem never left the palace unaccompanied, and now that Parvin inhabited a position of importance to the Sultan, she required her own personal chaperone. For the first time, he introduced himself. His name was Hyacinth. Many of the eunuchs had flower names. She studied him now, his wide eyes, his black lashes, his intelligent mouth.

"Why did you come forward to recite poetry that day?" she asked.

"To make certain that you would perform for the Alchemist. You were endangering yourself by disobeying him, and you were in my care."

"I don't think that's the only reason."

She was a more important person now. Everyone in the palace knew that the Sultan was taken with her, and they attributed the upcoming festivities to his newfound happiness. Hyacinth was not as much her superior as he had been before. He felt that he had to answer her honestly.

"I did it because I wanted to see you dance."

As soon as he said it, she worried that she had abused her new position and was afraid that she had humiliated him. But he didn't seem embarrassed by his admission; on the contrary, he seemed relieved. And something in her expression must have revealed that she was happy to hear him say it—not just because her suspicions were confirmed, but because she had hoped he would say exactly this. She began to cry, and she realized that she had been thinking of nothing but him for the last seven days, that during the Sultan's entertainments with her her own mind had traveled far away, to the man now known to her as Hyacinth. It struck her that her tears were tears of the joy of creation, that they were accompanied by the sweet, intense feeling that she had already imagined all of this, Hyacinth's standing there, gazing at her, and that there was a deep, satisfying pleasure in its fruition. She wondered if this wasn't always a part of falling in love, this feeling of living out a story that you have already secretly invented. She looked into his eyes and had the sense that the story she had written on her internal travels was about to continue in ways she could not have dreamt of, was about to leap out of her imagination and exist on its own. She felt as though she were the very story itself, the very letters and words dancing like shadows off the page. She had the feeling that she was entering the future.

So this is where they come from.

What?

Cymbals.

She had her head on his shoulder. He was stroking her hair.

From unrequited love, she said.

Then he kissed her. And she kissed him back.

At the northern end of the pleasure grounds between the Topkapi Saray and the seawalls along the Golden Horn were extensive gardens dotted with numerous small kiosks. Each consisted of three or four rooms with chimneys whose mantel trees were fashioned of silver and whose windows were glazed and protected with a gilt iron grill. The whole building was set with opals, rubies, emeralds, painted with flowers, and graced with inlaid works of porphyry, marble, jet, and jasper. The kiosks had many uses and one of the larger ones was used by the Chief Confectioner of the palace to soak and distill rose petals into an essence used for making the sweetmeat known to the West as Turkish delight. The building was called the Rose Pavilion.

This was where they came to meet each other during the celebration, and where they continued to meet for some time after. Hyacinth accompanied Parvin to the festivities hosted by the Sultan, and while her presence was required at night, there were many hours during the day when Murad took in games or theatricals or competitions and so she was free to travel about the gardens, accompanied by her chaperone, of course. Hyacinth had become friendly with the Chief Confectioner, who was also a eunuch captured in battle on the African shores, and he let the lovers in every afternoon, while he delivered his delicacies to the kitchen. The kiosk smelled so strongly of roses that they had to cover their faces at first, but eventually the odor became invisible to them, became the inevitable aroma of their time together. They brought blankets to spread on the floor and they swept aside the piles of discarded thorny stems. They had five afternoons in which to learn everything they could about each other—they didn't know what chance they would have to meet again—and so they talked and touched incessantly, while the rose petals slowly soaked inside the pavilion and, outside, the sun inched dispassionately down toward the sea.

The first afternoon they fell into each other hungrily, dangerously. They stared at each other with fascination and surprise, strangers but astonishingly familiar. They mouthed each other's names; later, she would laugh at his, because it seemed so out of keeping with his strength and because it had been given to him when he had been captured and taken as a eunuch and therefore seemed not really his name at all, but now she said it over and over. He said hers too, in the same mellow voice he had used to recite poetry, only he spoke it more softly, and he did not try to hide his emotion when his face trembled or his lips shook. His hands held her face in his, and she felt like a bird's egg: small and safe and about to be born. Her hands raced all over his body, taking him in through her fingertips. She explored daringly at first, and then, somewhat gingerly. She was unsure. But when she reached down, filled with trepidation, to where she had expected to find an absence, she was met with a presence that both overjoyed and shocked her. Here was the beginning of the future she had sensed. This was something she could not have invented.

He was not what she expected a eunuch to be. At first, she did not ask questions. She merely enjoyed the results of her misapprehension, and left it at that. But later, as they lay side by side in the Rose Pavilion, flower petals strewn across their blankets and crushed underneath them, a thorny stem captured in her long hair, she wondered aloud why he had not been treated like the others. She knew what happened to eunuchs. She knew that some of them were castrated before puberty, and that others, those who were taken later, usually in battle or in the slave trade, those were mutilated completely. A doctor in the palace checked the men every year, to make sure that nothing had grown back. It was considered essential to the eunuchs' purpose—the guarding and protecting of women—that they be uninterested in their charges, and therefore trustworthy. They also held many other positions of power within the palace, but the black eunuchs' chief responsibility was to watch over the harem. How could he have escaped the fate of the others? How had he maintained his manhood?

He smiled when she asked him, as if holding back a laugh. "Before I tell you," he said, "I want to know if it would have made a difference."

She thought for a moment. Then she said, "I fell in love with you when you grabbed my arm in the carriage. I didn't know it then, but I did. And I assumed you were like the others, so that answers your question. But am I happy I was wrong? Yes."

He explained that when he was captured they had brutalized his testicles, but he had run away before they could do anything more. They had found him, and brought him to the palace, but when they took him before the Kizlar Agha, the Chief of the Eunuchs, the man had been so taken with the new charge's beauty that he had instantly given him the name Hyacinth and declared that he would be his personal attendant. As soon as Hyacinth was alone with him, he told the Kizlar Agha that if he castrated him completely he would kill himself, and the Agha, already half in love with the boy, had acquiesced.

"Then why did he send you to take care of the women?"

"Once he realized that I would never return his feelings, he only wanted to make sure that I wasn't around the men. He was more jealous of them than of the women."

They both smiled when he said this, because the idea so completely contradicted their present state. Then they saw that the first pink lights of sunset were streaming into the kiosk and they knew that their time was ending.

"What was your real name?" she asked.

"Subbaharan," he said.

She had trouble pronouncing it, and it sounded to her like the name of someone unhappy, someone doomed. She touched his long eyelashes with her fingertips and said, "I like Hyacinth."

2005

It was dim in the room but Milo's eyes shone. They always seemed to reflect what little light there was. His face was close to hers and he was studying her, preparing to ask a question.

What did you do before this?

His tone of voice told her that this was the time when she could no longer avoid talking about herself. She pushed her hair behind her ear. She closed her eyes and opened them and took a breath.

I was a dancer. And then I wasn't.

What happened?

She tilted her head. She looked away and then back at him.

I had an injury.

What happened?

I lost someone very close to me. I was upset. I threw

myself into dancing and then I fell. From up high.
Onstage. I can't dance again.

She thought she might start to cry but she didn't.

So you are a shaman, he said, holding her close.

Your shaman, she said.

1623

The festivities ended and Hyacinth accompanied Parvin
back to the palace. He brought her to the Sultan's chambers where Kaya was waiting for her, and they had no privacy in which to say good-bye. They didn't know when
they would be able to see each other again. As he was leaving, he pressed a rose petal into her palm.

When Parvin opened her hand and looked at the
bruised petal, Kaya clucked and told her to forget him.

"They say you are going to be a Haseki," said Kaya, "the
Sultan's favorite. Then you will never go back to the Old
Palace."

"How can I be a Haseki? The Sultan knows I don't like
him. I'm just the one he enjoys right now. As long as I
don't have his baby, I'll be safe."

"Believe what you like," said Kaya, brushing Parvin's
hair. "But the talk in the Valide Sultan's suite is that you
will be a Haseki. Cheer up. You're going to be rich."

2005

Now it was dark. You could hear the faraway sounds of cars and the heaving of trucks going by in the night if you listened, but Honor and Milo weren't listening to anything but the story. They were working in the dark, following a moonlit trail, hunters in a green-black deepening forest, fishermen at sea.

Do you think she and Hyacinth will be together? she asked.

No, he said. This story is tragic. The Sultan will keep them apart.

Will she end up with Avedis?

Then his love won't be unrequited, and I told you, this one is tragic.

No, it would be. She loves Hyacinth.

1623

One day a eunuch arrived to take her to Avedis's workshop. It was an important occasion. None other than the Sultan himself was going to be present. The eunuch, who was not Hyacinth, explained that, as he understood it, although Avedis had not entirely completed his project for the Sultan it was almost finished and the metalsmith had requested to have Parvin dance for him in order to make the final touches and that the Sultan had only agreed to such a meeting if he were in attendance, because of course no one could view her dance without the express permission of the Sovereign. Parvin only half listened to the eunuch as he babbled on and didn't think to mention that she was in no mood to dance or that the thought of seeing that strange and unhelpful Alchemist again reminded her of the day that Hyacinth had stopped her from jumping out of the carriage. She missed him. She pulled her silk skirts tightly in her delicate hand and lifting her feet softly followed behind the eunuch as he skittered and wobbled across the palace grounds to Avedis's workshop. At one point she turned around to look for her love because she thought that she could sense his presence, but she saw nothing except lonely gardens, and she had no idea that she had missed him by an instant. His dark shape was hidden in the shadow of a wall, not twenty feet away from her.

Avedis had prepared an elaborate presentation, during which he said, as he told them what he was going to say, that he would reveal to them how he had discovered the secret formula for the making of cymbals. Not just any cymbals, but the ideal cymbals, the gleaming discs from which would ring the celestial music of the spheres. He stood up in his workshop, the dim light filtering through glass jars filled with jewel-colored liquids and flickering off the bronze cups lining the shelves reflecting onto him in a deep coppery color that made him appear like a bronze statue come to life. He was a tall, thin, wizardish-looking man with the unconsciously haughty and slightly silly air of an aspiring academic. He wore a long beard that lengthened his already long face and made his kind, sincere, searching eyes appear to be floating even higher in the lofty realm of the mystical than they actually were. He possessed a ridiculous hopefulness and his heart was visible on his face and Parvin, after getting over her disgust at having to sit beside the Sultan with her hand on his broad knee, was carried along by the rapturous recounting of Avedis's discovery. She was pulled into his narrative as if she were a drowned body being carried along underwater by a fast current, the details and turns of his story embedding themselves in her mind like twigs and leaves and pebbles catching in the twisting scarf of her long hair.

In the drama of his recounting his first vision of her dance (again that fateful day), which he couched in quasi-religious terms so as not to threaten or offend the Sultan, Avedis became swept up in his own story. He told his rapt audience about his own past, his apprenticeship as a metal-smith, his developing interest in alchemy, his promotion within the court, his devotion to the Sultan, and he worked his way onto the subject of the great city of Constantinople. A melting pot of cultures! he cried. He spoke now with deep, affecting emotion about the cosmopolitanism of his beloved home, how the Turks, Jews, Armenians, Persians, and so many others lived in harmony together and he paused to look gratefully at Murad. In this incredible melting pot, he said, made possible by the broad-mindedness of our noble leaders—and here the Sultan smiled, because he enjoyed flattery of any flavor and also because he was intelligent enough to appreciate that it was the brilliance of the Ottoman Empire, among many other insights, to recognize the value of many cultures living together in peace, in no small part because different kinds of people were good at and willing to engage in different kinds of work, which when administered wisely hugely benefited the economy. He may himself not have been a peace-loving or intellectual man, but he was not stupid. In this incredible melting pot, Avedis continued, I myself have been moved and softened and changed, like a piece of stone turning to gold in one of my own cauldrons, by so many disparate influences that I have been transformed! Transformed by a vision of beauty! And in the transformation of my own awareness of beauty I have been given the gift of inspiration. I have been inspired and enabled to create a vehicle for reproducing, in all its wondrous complexity, a wild, delicate, mysterious, and utterly simple sound: the sound of love.

And what are the components of this sound? First: Beauty, he said. And he picked up a piece of metal and a silver stick and struck it so that a clear and lovely note rang forth. Next, Desire: and he replaced the first piece of metal he had chosen for a shinier yet darker alloy, which he again struck with the stick. A lower, more deeply reverberating sound was released. And he did the same with the next three attributes: compassion, gentleness, selflessness, each had its own corresponding metal alloy. And then, he said: Freedom. I could go on and on, but let us stop at freedom. Freedom, I realized in my philosophical wanderings toward this sound, freedom is an essential component of love, perhaps the most important. Because in trying to keep, or hold, your beloved, one is acting not of love but possessiveness, need, selfishness. The sound of freedom was the most important sound for love, but where to find it? I pondered the object of my mission, the glorious Parvin, and I watched her dance. Here his eyes misted, and a muscle near his mouth twitched. I studied her spontaneous passionate dancing, and now the Sultan himself shifted uncomfortably in his seat, and I realized that for her freedom only existed in dance, in movement, in the abstract, because, of course, my dear Parvin was not free. A tear slid down his cheek. Parvin felt a chill. She desired to curl up into a tiny ball, but she stayed frozen. She stared at the hem of Avedis's left sleeve. The Sultan spoke up: Play the damn things! You boring fool!! He laughed, menacingly. Avedis nodded to a young apprentice, who brought over what appeared to be a plate covered by a shawl. Avedis pulled off the silk with a flourish. The Sultan's four bodyguards put their hands on the ends of their swords. There were two cymbals. He held one in each hand, and, unable to control himself, boldly went on: She has captured the wild elegance of freedom in her dance, but tragically, yes, tragically, she is not free. Here he stared at Parvin and let the cymbals collide. A sweet, soaring, light-dark sound, the color of sunlight striking a bloodred wine, engulfed the room.

My love, he said.

The Sultan looked at one of the guards and a rush of bodies pushed from the sides of the room inward toward Avedis. Suddenly, chaos. The Alchemist remained calm as the storm rushed toward him. He stood reveling in the reverberations of his love. Parvin sensed the Sultan's glare upon her and turned to glance back into his fury. He looked on her as he might look at a smear of shit underfoot. Then his face contorted into a different level of disgust, and under his eyes appeared half-moons bred from fear. Then again, his mouth opened and from the back of his dark throat he said: Another whore. Clutching his sword he strode forward into the crowd of bodies.

Parvin stared at Avedis as he was dragged out of his workshop, the cymbals dropping to the floor and clanging, before circling on their rims in a final, spiraling dance.

It seemed to her that the dark room was swallowing her up into one of its elixirs. She tried to stand but found herself frozen in place. She felt a familiar hand grip her arm. Follow me, a low voice said. The voice betrayed nothing as it led her through a dark passageway and out of Avedis's workshop and just as they entered the twilit gardens Parvin lifted her head from staring at the ground in front of her feet and saw her dark handsome beloved striding purposefully forward, her hand in his. I have been instructed to dispose of you, he said, turning around quickly. Hyacinth looked in her eyes as if to say: Everything will be fine. But she couldn't be sure. The gardens bled into a palace stairway. The two figures made a sharp left onto the stairs. A crowd of the Sultan's henchmen passed them, dragging Avedis. His cries faded away as they hurried off.

We were wrong.
  We were.
  She won't end up with Avedis.
  It doesn't look like it.
  She was putting on her coat and turning on the lights.
  It's time to go. The nurse is coming.
  Don't go.
  She stopped buttoning her coat.
  I'll be here tomorrow.
  She kept buttoning.
  Don't go.
  I have to go.

·

When Joe and Vivian said good-bye inside the car it was a Sunday afternoon in Brooklyn and the sun was out. He held her awkwardly in the front seat and she was crying and with his eyes closed he remembered when he'd seen her cry before, that day at the museum. He remembered the way her tears had been reflected in the glass, drops of gold sliding downward to the jungle floor. He heard the hollow sounds of children's voices echoing in the vast room. He felt Vivian's restrained yet passionate presence standing next to him. He saw her face on the body of a tiger.

CHAPTER THIRTEEN

1936

Pearl stood in the doorway holding the door open when he came home. She was wearing a pretty blouse and her smart skirt and she had a dish towel in her hand. Her face was glistening with perspiration and her hair was pulled back at the sides and then loose in back. Her face looked young like a twelve-year-old girl's but her hands were thin and veined and he never liked to look at her knuckles. They showed how hard she had to work. Her wedding band swam around on her finger like a Life Saver. Her ankles were crossed and she was wearing heels. She almost always wore heels. He could smell a pot roast in the oven and through the doorway he could see the living room in a haze of afternoon light, the simple furniture blurred and softened and welcoming and beyond that a shaft of late sun slicing through the kitchen and he could glimpse it and it looked like home.

At dinner she said, How did it go? Did the band like you?

They did. Nice guys.

He took a forkful of vegetables. He chewed them thoroughly. He chewed for a long time.

Do they have any gigs coming up?

A few. Out of town.

She was getting him more roast.

Anything overseas?

Possibly. But that work is harder to get, you know. Not as many liners crossing these days.

That's such a shame Joe. It's such good money.

She smoothed her skirt and sat back down.

What'll we do?

We'll be fine, he said.

He took her hand across the table.

Only another year until I graduate. I'm doing well this semester. I'll be getting legal work soon.

I'm glad you're feeling optimistic, she said. Because I went ahead and bought these.

She took two tickets from her pocket and put them in his hand. They were for Count Basie Christmas Eve at the Roseland Dance Palace. He put them on the table and stared at them.

Pearl . . .

We deserve to have some fun, she said.

He held her hand and looked at her.

I know how much you like to go dancing, she said. Remember when we used to go? I know I'm not the best dancer, but . . .

He kept holding her hand and looking at her.

I'm not too shabby, she said.

2005

So who was he?

Who?

The person you lost.

She had been far away: the Bosphorus, a yellow kitchen, Roseland.

He was a journalist.

What kind?

A war correspondent.

I see.

She looked down into his back and saw the muscles tense slightly under his shoulder blades. It was where his wings would have been.

I met him when I first moved back to New York, around the time I first found work dancing. We lived in the same building. His studio was the floor above mine. He was a little older. He was out of college a few years.

A college boy. A fancy college, I bet. Smart, I bet.

Yes.

He took a deep breath. Keep talking, he said.

He was writing pieces about fires in the Bronx or waste transfer stations. He was on the Metro desk. He was just starting out. I was just starting out too. I was in a show, Off Broadway. It was doing well. We were talking about finding a bigger place.

She wasn't thinking now she was just talking and she put her hand on his neck. Then suddenly he turned his head and she saw the muscle turn in his neck and it was like a long stretch of sand curving ahead she was walking along a beach in early May the air still stung and the sun threw out a cold unwanted light. The tide pulled things away. She was walking with Sam near his parents' summerhouse but his parents were away they were always away and he said that he thought they should be together. He came up to her and pulled her close. Her hair blew in front of her eyes. The ocean was gray it had no blue in it and no green in it just gray and molten an almost colorless expanse of moving liquid and to her it looked beautiful that day she felt safe.

She kept her hand on his neck and she saw things she had not wanted to see: Sam in a restaurant the waiter hovering and then sliding away as Sam was telling her that they would be sending him it was a big step it was a vote of confidence it was very important for his career. She saw Sam's parents at another dinner this time a restaurant with many waiters and his parents were very polite to her, too polite, she could tell they didn't take her seriously even though her background was good but what had she done with it? She hadn't gone to college she was a dancer her family was from New York but where was her mother exactly? Yes, they had heard of the college where she taught but they quickly changed the subject and asked Sam more about his plans. She had wanted to say that they weren't really Sam's plans they were plans that other people, institutions, governments, and countries had made for him but she knew she would sound young and foolish and immature. His father was boyish and had been successful in local politics. His mother came from so much money she could afford to look unfashionable and she seemed basically kind but she would never have wanted anything like this dancer for her son and she seemed eerily excited that he was being sent into another world because he would move on from this infatuation. Of course she must have been terrified but to Honor she seemed like someone so rich for so long that it wouldn't necessarily occur to her that anything bad could happen. Later, Honor thought that she was wrong. She realized that what she had observed was an entirely public performance and that she had absolutely no idea what someone like that would think or feel. At the service his mother had looked like somebody who had been pieced together from different bodies. Her eyes did not look like each other. Her head seemed attached to the wrong person. She didn't see anyone or look at anyone and it was as if she had never met Honor. Honor signed the book along with everyone else.

Honor gripped Milo's neck tighter. She saw Sam with a different face: brown skin and his hair in a black scarf. He had been blond, fair, skin pink from the desert sun. They told him he stood out too much. He was too easy a target. They told him to get makeup and darken his skin. He wrote to her on the back of a Do Not Disturb sign that the brown cream would stain his clothes and rub off from his neck. His neck she could picture his neck inside one of his loose button-down shirts. In New York he dressed like the rich boy he was, but messy. She saw his neck it was strong but not tough he was not tough and when she had heard he had to disguise himself she thought that there was no disguising this kind of difference. He was brave and he was confident and he thought he could hide but he was not devious or savvy or cunning enough to pretend he was someone he wasn't. He couldn't even lie.

In the end though it was not his disguise that saved him

or gave him away. He wasn't a hero or a coward. They pulled the truck over. They killed everyone. It didn't matter what he looked like.

Do you see what I see?

The truck, he said.

Yes, she said.

I'm sorry.

She took her hand away and said, That's what I lost. That, and a lot of other things.

You'll tell me about those another day, he said.

Maybe, she said.

Then one day they told him that he was getting better and could go outside and could have visitors sit with him outside. There was a yard with some benches. It was spring again. It was cold. He asked her if she would come as a visitor. She asked him if he ever had any other visitors. He said, No. There's no one to come visit. So many visions, she said. So few visitors.

She'd never seen him wearing a coat before. She brought a present. She gave him the little box.

Don't get mad this time. It's just a present, not a party.

I won't, he said.

It was a watch.

I noticed you never wore one, she said. Do you already have one?

I used to. This is beautiful.

He put it on.

You're not going to rip it off and throw it across the street are you?

No. I'm never going to take it off.

She was on a bench. He wheeled closer to her. He kissed her. They held hands in the cold. A bird bounced around on the dirt. The clouds looked like they were waiting in the sky.

I'm going to use it to time myself when I do my exercises.

Honor allowed herself a smile.

They tell me you're doing well, she said.

I think I am. They say I've become more responsive. He gave a sheepish handsome grin.

You're going to stand up and walk for me?

I'm going to do more than that.

He looked right into her and through her and she thought she could see into him straight into his head and then through him past this building past this city someplace else.

What are you going to do?

Dance.

And one day he did walk. He walked a step. Then he walked more until he walked the length of the corridor. He walked by himself to their room. He walked right up to her and he took her in his arms and he held her up and he put her on the table.

1936

Vivian went to hear him play. There were planets turning in the cigarette smoke that swirled in the yellow light. The red tips of the fingers of the hostesses clicked against the little table when they cleared her drink. Another one, honey? they asked through dark lips. She ordered another but she didn't drink it.

Onstage he tilted slightly backwards and looked taller and thinner and his shirt stuck to him when he began to sweat. Then he leaned forward and the strap hung around his neck and his strong neck hung low and he looked solemn and calm like a horse in a field. Then he lifted only his head back and the moaning low music he had been making flew out from him in a smoky ribbon and circled in the air and it spiraled up to the pitch black of the balcony and it kept streaming heavenward and crying in the night and it was a long desperate animal howling and she knew that things would never be as easy as this again.

CHAPTER FOURTEEN

Joe knocked on the door. He walked in and Pearl was standing in front of the dresser facing the speckled mirror. She was looking down and so her face was absent from the reflection. She was fiddling with the clasp on her bracelet and she still hadn't put on her makeup. She was half dressed in her slip that was already wrinkled and her filmy stockings.

Can I help you? he said.

I'm having so much trouble with this, she said, not looking up.

He came up and put his arms around her from behind and closed the clasp so quickly it seemed a kind of magic.

Thank you, she said, still not looking up.

Is everything all right?

Now she looked at him. Her eyes seemed tired and small.

I don't know, she said. But she did know. Then she said: I'm not feeling well.

She walked over to the bed and sat down.

You seemed okay a little while ago.

I know. But I'm not now. My head hurts. Maybe it's the flu. I'm so sorry. I know how much you were looking forward to this.

I'm sorry you're not feeling well. He was ready. He had on a suit and his best black shoes.

Then she stood up and ran to the bathroom. He held her hair out of her face. He offered to stay home.

No, Joe, you should go. Why don't you see if Bud will go with you? He's on his own tonight.

It was Christmas Eve. Outside there was a deep stillness and the neighborhood felt empty. Random noises shot through the darkness up to the window from time to time, a car honk, a child's voice, suddenly piercing the blanket of quiet.

I can't leave you home like this.

You can't stay with me either. You'll be miserable. You'll make me miserable, she said, smiling. She was still in her slip with her bracelet still on and it rattled against the kettle when she poured water to make tea.

Go, she said. I wouldn't feel right if you stayed. And when you come back you can tell me all about it.

When he called Vivian's house her mother answered and she sounded weary and then surprised and delighted as if this would be the most exciting event of her evening. He was after all a distant relative by marriage and she was always happy to hear from family. He heard her call

Vivian and he could imagine the dim rooms with dark rugs and the carved old-world furniture. He could see Vivian reading next to a lamp. She would be surprised to hear from him. She would think he had gone out for the holiday evening with Pearl. She had known about the plan and she had also asked him not to call so often. They had tried to stay away. She had said she didn't want to see him if he couldn't tell Pearl and so far he hadn't. He couldn't. He had tried once or twice but the words were trapped in his head like dice in a cup and the hand wouldn't come off the top. But tonight he felt sure Vivian loved him. He could see her look up from her reading and hear his name and without thinking her body would bring her to him. He pictured her as she contained her pleasure. He saw her mother handing her the telephone. He pictured her mother walking off down a dim hall. He pictured the old man lying under heavy sheets in the bedroom, his vibrancy turned in on itself and his stillness a kind of ancient unwavering judgment. For a moment Joe felt afraid. And then it passed.

On Broadway a row of buildings that sat low and drab during the day were lit up like demented birthday cakes at night. The signs on the roofs blared with red and white and the words in gigantic black letters or scripted in flowing light spelled out the names of bandleaders or movie stars and biggest of all were the names of the places themselves like billboards for imaginary worlds. Loew's Mayfair, Lindy's restaurant, the Paradise, the Strand, the Winter Garden, the Rivoli, Casa Manana. The Cotton Club, the Brass Rail, the Roxy, the Capitol, the Continental, and Roseland. Just a few blocks up at Fifty-sixth Street stood the Broadway Tabernacle. It had been a theater but was now a church. Vivian was waiting for Joe on the sidewalk. The specks of metal in the pavement lifted up and seemed to glitter in midair. Everything glittered.

It was more beautiful than he had expected. A universe with the rules suspended, made for dancing, the music blowing through the crowded lobby. He helped her with her coat and handed it over the little table to the hat-check girl and took the small piece of painted wood with the black numbers on it that she handed to him. He felt the smooth wood between his fingers and pushed it in his pocket. He fumbled in his jacket for the tickets. He was holding the two tickets in his slightly trembling hand pressing forward with the crowd to get inside when he thought he saw someone he knew from law school who would know Pearl and he turned his head suddenly very close to Vivian's and told her she looked beautiful and handed the tickets to the ticket taker whose foot was tapping a beat against the floor.

A half hour later a horn sounded from backstage to signal that the main act would be coming soon. They had been listening to the opening band and were still waiting. Because it was Christmas Eve some revelers wore Santa hats or had brought bells to jingle and now they filled the silence between the orchestras with laughing and occasional jingling, a plaintive jubilance, a maudlin symphony. Joe and Vivian did not have bells and were not wearing hats and they stood amidst the revelers and then they snaked their way through the crowd and stood off to the side. He held her in his arms in a dark corner of the ballroom. Is this okay? he said.

She looked up at him and two streams of light seemed to rise toward him from her eyes. He reached for the wall next to her head with his hand. Above her right eye there was a lifting of the lashes and the brow that gave her a questioning, needing expression. In the left eye there was only a green spun with blue and yellow. Nothing wondering there. The calm poise of the left eye made it hard to distinguish the longing in the right eye and for a moment it made him distrust his instinct that she loved him. But it was too late to change anything. He put both his hands against the wall and began to kiss her. She kissed him back.

Suddenly, he heard the cover of the piano keys lift up across the room above the now dwindling sound of the bells and the muted brush of heels on the dance floor. He turned his head to look toward the stage and her lips grazed his cheek. There was no one there yet. Just a body gliding offstage behind the curtain, someone setting up. He turned back and kissed her again. Then the lights dimmed. His heart was beating in his head and her lips felt raw. He took her hand and pulled her back onto the dance floor.

She let him lead her back among the crowd and followed close. Outside somewhere in the streets beyond Roseland a siren wailed. A drunk cried out in the illuminated night. Joe realized that he could not have heard these things unless the ballroom had gone completely silent. He opened his hand slowly against her back and felt her shoulder blade slide beneath his touch. She leaned closer and her skin moved under his hand. Her dress was cut low in back and he felt her smoothness. He pulled her closer and gripped her dress. The lights changed again. Joe

watched the spotlights turn on with his eyes ablaze. When
they had turned on fully he suddenly saw the band enter
from the side and take the stage. He saw the night unfold
slowly before him. The gleam of the instruments shining
in his eyes. The Count's raised arm slightly tilted toward
the band. The fingers slightly touching in a snap held mo-
tionless in the air and the band's brass flung upward
against the satin backdrop. The fingers snapped and from
every corner the room swung.

Joe pulled her closer into an embrace and they began to
dance. He thought the swinging would subside but the
band would not let go of it and they whirled him with it
again and again. She fell into him fending away the sounds
but the music blared and he saw her truly scared for the
first time her head leaning into him seeking him out like
something rushing away from a fire. He held on to her and
the floor seemed to be spinning underneath them. In a second of calm he brushed the hair from her eyes and took
her face in his hands and he kissed her on the forehead.
She seemed surprised. She was trying to hang on to him.

The next thing Joe knew he was leading her off the dance
floor. She was back against the wall. He stepped forward
toward her, pressing her, and although they weren't dancing they were still spinning. They were in the dark. There
was no light here. She moved her head to the side trying to
get away. She gripped his forearm as if to push him off her
but he held it firm. She tried again to move her head away
but he was coming closer. He could smell her. She was
wearing a sweet languorous foreign perfume. She closed
her eyes and leaned her head finally against the wall. Joe

dropped his hands on either side of her ribs and he stared
through the darkness into what he could see of her eyes.
She didn't say anything. He leaned into her against the
wall and ran his tongue along the corner of her mouth. He
pressed against her and his legs wanted to bend crookedly
to the floor and collapse but somehow he held them
straight. The music had swung them here and it went on
blithely swinging and it occurred to him that this happy
romantic rhythm would kill them both. The lights
changed again and he could see her eyes.

We should stop, Joe, she said.

We should go someplace else. I know where.

And they left Roseland.

CHAPTER FIFTEEN

It happens every night: the sound of cymbals reminds him that it is impossible to keep time.

The Count and the reflections of the Count on the instruments sway slightly when he lifts his hand. He turns in time to the beat and his image dances along the line of brass, so that although he is gracefully and confidently conducting his orchestra, he appears to be imprisoned inside the music.

He nods his head. The room swings.

Usually, his band is vibrant and unafraid, but tonight they are overtired and underrehearsed. He hears the inevitable imperfection in their playing almost as soon as they take the stage. A subtle shift in tempo, an awkward note. When the illusion that his ensemble operates as a single consciousness is broken, he feels a sadness that verges on desperation, a deep disappointment with humanity. But then as quickly as the trombones swerve direction or the trumpets lunge, he forgets his philosophical troubles.

His mind itself swings. Like a screen door his mother used to say. Like long hair on a lazy girl.

He is a perfectionist in his head but a pragmatist at heart. He has them, for a moment he holds them in his spell. He feels the room lighten, as if the people on the dance floor had levitated to the height of the chandeliers, bubbles in a glass of champagne. He has them and he feels that as long as there is music playing, it is possible to forgive the world.

It is 1936. There is much to forgive. But he is lucky, he is making his New York debut on Christmas Eve at the Roseland Ballroom.

Just then, as suddenly as he recaptures the flow, the band loses it, and he is thrown back to the beginning. He knows now that they will have a rough night. There are critics here. The reviews will be mediocre.

He notices a beautiful face in the crowd. A dangerous face. There is always one of those.

But by the time the articles go to press, he won't care about the critics. He will have ridden the crashing waves of cymbals a thousand times, and he will have lost himself over and over again, perspiring so much that it will feel as if he had literally been tossed around in the ocean. And then, finally, he will have found a kind of safety. A safety in loss, a safety in losing. Losing control and keeping it, the essential mystery of swing.

The face dissolves and resurrects itself behind a column. There is a body, too. Always one of those.

.

Years later, he will remember this night not as a fiasco of missed opportunity or an evening of more than minor humiliation, but as one of the highlights of what will become an illustrious, a shimmering career. He will close his eyes and see a man's hand pressed flat against a woman's shoulder, guiding her to the dance floor. He will roll his eyes backwards and recall the insinuating angle of a cigarette. A necklace splintering light like the eyes of a madman. A river of bodies, gliding noiselessly through time.

He will remember the moments when his orchestra seemed to conjure itself, when it achieved the purity of a single mind. A mind in which many different voices conversed, argued, flirted, seduced, philosophized, all within the limits of one being. He will remember the drums, he will never forget the drums, and he will remember the faces, the unconditional love he felt for those faces. He will not remember the uneasy feeling of failure, the brush with oblivion, the premonition of unrequited life. He will only remember the memory.

Later, when they ask him about that first night at Roseland, he will lean back and he will close his eyes and he will say:

You should have seen us. You should have been there.

Joe

He took her to the apartment of a drummer he knew, someone who wouldn't be home. He remembered where he kept the key. It was in a planter in the hallway. A dying plant opposite the elevator. His friend would be traveling. The apartment was dark and empty.

She said she didn't believe that he would ever leave Pearl. He said he would. It would be very difficult, but he would. She said that tonight she would believe him. He said that he would take care of her. He said that she could trust him.

They were lying on the floor. She wouldn't go into the bedroom. The light of a December morning came up cold and very white and her skin looked almost silver.

Later, she said: I didn't think that the band was all that great.

Her head was resting on his chest and he looked down at her and smiled.

You're impossible, he said.

No really, she said. They sounded off of their game.

I don't know. I thought they were good, he said. But I might have been distracted.

Milo

One day Honor realized that he would not always need to live in this place, that he was getting better, that she had helped him. She took comfort in the fact that even when he seemed to be guiding her through the past, she must have been doing something to help him move toward the future.

Still, although he could walk again, Milo would never

lie on his back. He would not give up his secret. Stories yes, but never his secret.

Tell me what happened, she said.

It's just another story, he said.

It's not just a story, she said. It's you.

PART THREE

In the slaughterhouse of love,
Only the best are killed . . .
Don't run away from this dying.

—RUMI

CHAPTER SIXTEEN

It was almost funny. First Pearl told him with tears in her eyes and an optimistic yet resigned expression. Then Vivian told him the same thing, only with a terrified, stricken look on her face. He had two women depending on him more than ever and he could do nothing other than walk along the river with his hands in his pockets wondering how he could get on another liner not only to escape his predicament but more important, to make some money. He reassured himself by thinking that Pearl would probably not make it again this time and then he despised himself for having such a thought. And Vivian, she was not ready for this but perhaps it would settle the matter once and for all; he would have to be with her now. It had been weeks and he had still not spoken to Pearl about Vivian. But once Pearl saw that he and Vivian would be a family, he surmised, she would have some sympathy. Again he was disgusted with the way his mind worked. Why should Pearl care about his happiness? Why would he imagine that she wouldn't be sickened by his betrayal and hate him for it? Of course she would not wish him and Vivian well. He was insane to hope for that. Worse, he was a terrible person for thinking of leaving her. Ever. But most of all now.

His mind swung. He was leading the beat in his head with the percussion of his heart. His head and his heart were no match for time. He had been swept up in the music and now the music had swept him aside. He was just someone in the midst of the music of history. History conducted by a bandleader. History, conducting life.

But what was so historical about his problem? It was a timeless dilemma, no specific circumstances had given rise to it, just romance and passion and stupidity. He didn't care about seeing himself as important or unimportant, but suddenly it occurred to him that if there hadn't been a Depression he wouldn't have been playing on ships, if he hadn't been playing on ships he wouldn't have met Vivian on the dock, if he hadn't met Vivian . . . But this was such shallow, faulty reasoning that he nearly laughed into the wind. No, his problem was simply his. Still, there was the music, the current of which had carried him here. And there was a moment in time that had given rise to that music, a moment and a music that had seemed so isolated from history. No one thought about the fact that swing music really started in Constantinople at a time of great cosmopolitanism and cultural exchange. No one thought that what seemed so American had come from an Armenian alchemist in seventeenth-century Turkey. Only Vivian was smart enough to think about something like that.

Thinking about it now made him suspect that although his problems seemed exclusively his, perhaps they did go further back than he could imagine. What he didn't consider was how far forward they might travel. That they might reverberate through time like the sound of cymbals across a dance hall, that he did not contemplate.

The wind stirred up the river. There were whitecaps today, streaks of white like dashes across the blue, making a moving poetry out on the water. He wondered what Vivian would have said about that. He thought about her, scared and burdened and feeling alone in the dim house with the heavy rugs. He thought about Pearl, hopeful for the sixth time. He thought about what a spectacular mess he had made. He thought that maybe finally he was going to have a child. Or two. What this kind of beginning would lead to he had no idea. What kind of person or people would thrive or wither from such an origin as this he had no idea. He couldn't read the future. He felt ashamed at the way this unborn child's life had begun and nevertheless proud that if his actions were going to ride on the waves of the future that they would ride in the form of life. Life, he figured, had been riding these waves for centuries and would always find some kind of rhythm. No, there was no way to hold on to time. He would just throw it up in the air like a smiling baby. He would swing it in his arms.

2005

I never liked him, Honor said.

He's a prick, Milo said, but I feel for him. He doesn't know any better.

He should.

She pushed some hair out of her face with the back of her hand.

This doesn't sound like you. You're usually so forgiving.

She had finished on his back and she was looking at nowhere. He sat up.

What is it? he said.

I don't feel for him, she said. Something's changed. I don't feel like I have to forgive everyone. He should know better. He's ruining lives, she said.

He's not killing anyone, Milo said.

We don't know that. And killing isn't the only way to ruin lives.

No, but it's a good one, he said.

He got down from the table and started to put on his shirt.

He was supposed to be moving out soon. He was walking. He was ready, they said. She was helping him find a place to live. He would need to stay nearby for a while to keep up his rehabilitation, so he could not go back yet to Maine. She was happy. He would stay close. They didn't talk about it, but it was clear that they would stay close.

When he finished getting dressed and she was ready to

go, he held the door for her and they walked down the hall together.

1969

When she was rummaging around the apartment she found the photograph. It was under the table on top of a pile of papers. Iris saw them looking up at her from a skewed angle as if they were watching her on the ceiling while they lay in bed. She knew the photograph would be there someplace because she had sent it to the photographer. She had sent it with a note that said: "Remember us?"

Now she had come to take other pictures away. She felt no qualms about taking them; she felt they were rightly hers. She thought of the pictures as a kind of shadow self, her ghostly twin. They represented an alternate life, what she might have been, not a photographer but a photograph. A subject, an object, an object of affection if there had not been the photographs. The photographs reflected her missing self, the negative that she felt herself to be. She saw them everywhere, scattered carelessly around the room. The old ones had been black and white but these were Kodachrome and infused with the melancholy yellows and reds of the era, the muted bleached-out colors of a city afternoon. A child on the subway looking up at an advertisement, her mother staring down at her, their bodies twisted both toward and away from each other. A group of children in the park, one persuading the others of something, a face gripped with determination and laced with contempt. A little boy lying down on the sidewalk looking skyward with a carefree arrogance. All children in every one of them, but none innocent, each individual. The artist had seen every one of her subjects as a person and had not shied away from the humor and terror just below the surface of their faces and lives. Iris glanced at them quickly, her ink and chemical siblings, and threw them into a shopping bag. She gathered contact sheets and rolls of film. She left the wedding photograph where it was. She left.

Out on the street with her vigilante shopping bag she felt watched, as if people would know what she was carrying, what she had done. Then, overeducated girl that she was, she thought how ironic that was, that she would feel herself watched, looked at, as if she herself were a picture. She had turned herself into a photograph! Perhaps that way she could get some attention! She smiled to herself and looked quickly to the side before crossing the street. It was warmer out than she had expected and her feet were swelling slightly in her shoes. She was getting blisters. But still she continued walking, afraid to stop, to lose momentum. It was a long walk home. She calculated: from Twelfth Street uptown, over seventy blocks, more than three miles. There was a manic energy to her movements, her legs scissoring exceptionally quickly, her head switching side to side to check for traffic at every crosswalk, strands of her hair flying as she propelled herself home. Home, where the baby would be, where Alex would not be, yet. Iris tried to construct a warm and welcoming feeling from the notion of home, but she had never actually experienced that. Even as a child, although home had been friendly and her parents doting in their way, home had never felt like a place where one could actually be understood. Her sense of not belonging, she later grew up to believe, was what everyone felt, and so she did not dwell on it, but of course it hurt, it confused her, and then when there was an answer, or something to pin it all on, she clung to it. The bag was getting heavier.

She stopped. She put the bag down. It was a large lavender thick paper bag from Bergdorf Goodman with an image of black silhouetted shoppers parading at an angle up the side. Iris had saved it from the purchase of a new dress. A crocheted dress, very of-the-moment, something Alex would like and yet not fully appreciate. Certainly he would not appreciate the price. She rubbed her hand. The twisted paper handles of the bag had dug into her palm, creating new lines, a new future, she thought for a moment. Then, and this was the way her mind worked, she seemed to enter that new future and for an instant the past disappeared. She was standing on a street corner with an overstuffed Bergdorf's bag at her feet, a breeze blowing over from Madison Square Park tangling up her hair, and she had no past. She saw herself as if in a black-and-white photograph taken from the window of a building nearby, seen from slightly above, a woman on the street, lost, or so it would appear, rubbing her hand, the wind coming from behind her, blowing her hair forward, she a silhouette, yet unlike the figures on her bag not parading but standing still, held in place by the wind and the force of forgetting, a person caught in time. She was too intelligent to not see herself but not wise enough to help herself.

A photograph, she thought suddenly, is like an ink and chemical memory in the mind of the subject being photographed. I am standing here, she thought, and a picture of me would be a picture of what I can imagine, as if the image itself were lifted from the mind of the woman being photographed. I should write an essay about that idea, she thought. And then she picked up the bag and kept walking.

1937

Joe and Pearl sat in the living room after dinner with the lamp on. Outside the winter night had long ago gone dark. He was studying and had his books piled up on the low coffee table, his feet up next to them, crossed and in socks. She was knitting and her fingers moved with furious intent, whipping around each other and sliding the needles through the yarn with a machinelike choreography and precision. He asked if she was making something for the baby. She said no that the yarn she was using was too rough. She was making him a scarf.

2005

Milo lay on his bed and touched the thin sheets, the lonesome blanket, the sandpaper wall. He would miss this pathetic bed. He looked up at the ceiling and today there was no swinging house. No saxophone case coming through the plaster. They had given him a date when he could leave and suddenly life seemed very simple and earthbound. He had hoped for this and dreamt about it. He had talked about it with Honor during their visits in the yard. He had worked hard in physical and occupational therapy to be able to reach this day. Now the day felt frightening in its ordinariness. The ceiling blank and cold and white. In moments of calm he felt as though he were impersonating a normal human being, someone who wouldn't be frightened by an empty room or made despairing by the thought of losing that room. He was just feeling an ordinary sadness, he told himself. It did not have to go any further than that.

He turned on his side. His legs felt strong but tired. He had worked them hard this morning. He looked at the wall. He saw shades of lavender and pink in the light on the wall. No yellowing kitchen. No city lights. Just the color of this day in this room. Then his hand reached out to the wall and he saw his fingers touch the wall and he saw them stroking the wall and he saw them touching the wall as if he were pressing keys. Keys on a saxophone, keys on a typewriter. He looked at his hand and it was touching nothing, a blank wall, a blank page. He tried to take it away but he knew that he wouldn't. The pull was too strong. Reaching out to the wall was like reaching back inside to something long gone and sorely missed, something that had abandoned him the way the stars abandon the city sky because there is too much reflected light, something there if he could only see it. If the city could shatter and the stars could return, that was what he was reaching for.

A black case moved through the wall and sat on the bed. It opened to reveal a typewriter.

1969

Iris put the shopping bag in the back of the closet. She moved the typewriter case in front of it. She let Geraldine go and went to check on the baby. Soon, Alex would be coming home for dinner from the hospital. She would have to start cooking.

She changed her dress and put on different tights. It was 1969 and she wore dark tights nearly every day. Her hair was brown and straight and parted in the middle. She wore it chin length and when she had it done it curled under her pretty chin. She had green eyes and black glasses which only accentuated her prettiness. She had changed into a navy blue dress which hit her at the knee and she put on her favorite amber necklace. She put on lipstick even though she was only going to the kitchen to make dinner and she had to stand tiptoe at the small porcelain sink with its thin metal legs to see her face in the square glass medicine cabinet. The baby cried. She ran to get her.

In the kitchen the baby sat in her high chair eating pureed vegetables and wearing a bib. Iris talked to her while she prepared dinner from a book called *Never in the Kitchen When Company Arrives*. They were not having a dinner party tonight but they had many and she had become dependent on this book. They had dinner parties to help restore Alex's reputation. He had had trouble since the trial. He was only now beginning to get referrals. Mostly he took whatever surgeries came his way at the hospital, but he was not in high repute. He had to defer to younger doctors, doctors who were less well educated, doctors he didn't like. He came home withdrawn. He read the paper.

Iris looked out the little window in the kitchen. They lived on the twentieth floor of a postwar building on Second Avenue. It was one of the tallest buildings around and from it she could see the East River and the Empire State Building. It was a fancy apartment for them and too expensive, certainly her mother thought so, but they had taken it anyway right after the trial ended and he had found work and they had had the baby. They needed something to lift their spirits. Of course, having a child lifted their spirits, but it was also difficult and exhausting and it strained their already weakening bond. They didn't laugh as much together, although one night only a couple of weeks after becoming parents they had decided to go bowling only to realize that they could not bring the baby and had not even thought about getting a babysitter. This made them both laugh. Being parents did not come naturally to them and it was a time in which they could not bring a baby out easily and so they found themselves home much of the time and Iris was grateful for the view.

Still, as the months went on the apartment seemed boxy and low-ceilinged and she regretted having bought a white couch and a white marble table. They were the height of fashion but she craved color. One day she decided to paint one wall in the hallway a dark red. When Alex came home she was smiling and there was Beethoven playing on the record player and the baby was cooing with her feet shooting up in the air like fat flowers and Alex said you cannot do something like that without asking me and how much do you think all this paint costs and do you ever think about anyone besides yourself? She stood up and the red paint dripped onto the parquet floor. That's when she saw a look on his face that she had never seen before and it was livid and his eyes were widened in astonishment and rage. Years later she recognized that he had not been looking at her but at something deep inside his own brain, yet at the time he was appalled by her and she did not know how it had happened and it was growing bigger and coming closer like a storm.

This was the time when she thought about her life and she decided that she knew what had been the problem. She found the famous photographer's address in the phone book. She wrapped the wedding picture in newspaper and mailed it to the building in Greenwich Village. She waited for a response that never came. She sat at the typewriter and tried to compose a more thoughtful letter than the hostile note that she had sent with the photograph, but the words would not come. She sat there and hours passed in a flicker. Her whole past scrolled through her mind and she thought about why she had written that fateful letter to the newspaper, how she had become someone so headstrong and impulsive, what would have happened if she had been raised differently, how her marriage would have worked out if she had only been understood so long ago. The baby cried. She went to get her.

Then one day she spent too much money and he was angrier than she had ever seen him. She had been walking home along Madison Avenue and had not been able to resist a new dress for her birthday and besides he gave her such a small allowance, too little to run the house, and she was working so hard taking care of the baby, taking classes, taking his clothes to the cleaner and she hated the way she sounded but more she was frightened of the look on his face as if she could control everything she did, didn't he know by now that she was the kind of person who would be struck still on a street corner, someone for whom time had no real meaning, a person whose mind was not quite like everyone else's, and it was all an affront to him instead of a cry for closeness she missed him she was lonely. Not long after that she heard about the photographer's upcoming show at the Museum of Modern Art. Iris had worked at the museum right after college and still had friends there. She had the address of the brownstone in her change purse.

She could not have those pictures hanging in a museum when those pictures should have been hers. They were more than hers, they were *her.*

Pearl

Her eyes were red and her nose was red and a strand of hair was stuck to her cheek. She was in bed when he got home. She didn't have to tell him that it had happened again. Joe held her and he felt her neck wet with tears and the lace on her slip wet with tears and he thought that the only thing more painful than unrequited love was unrequited life.

CHAPTER SEVENTEEN

The waitress left two cloudy glasses of water on the table and walked away. Joe took out a cigarette although he rarely smoked and he lit it and turned his head to blow out the smoke. Vivian sat with her coat wrapped tightly around her, a scarf still at her throat. She looked pale.

She looked out the window onto an empty lot. They were at a diner on Eighth Avenue in the Thirties. She did not want to risk seeing anyone either of them knew and he had eaten in this all-night coffee shop after gigs. The table was edged with aluminum and the booths smelled of fresh leather. He reached out to take her hand across the Formica but she left it loosely around her glass. Her other hand was in her pocket.

Do you want anything to eat?

No thanks. I don't have any appetite.

Shouldn't you have something?

I'm not hungry.

Outside it began to snow. First the gentlest confetti swirled down one at a time like the last remnants of a celebration. Then they began to accumulate and the swirls grew thicker and looked like the long white hair of angels falling down.

The waitress returned and Joe ordered a coffee and a slice of pie. He knew that he wouldn't eat the pie but he felt bad for the girl and thought that he should order something. When it came the pie sat uneaten on the table, a sweet stark reminder of his foolishness.

He blew out more smoke. He took a sip of coffee. He accepted that she wasn't going to hold his hand.

I told her, he said.

Her right eye trembled. Her left eye stayed calm.

After what happened we both felt like we could discuss some things. He paused. She said she would like for us to be happy. You and me.

She looked back out the window. The snow was coming now in what appeared to be great heaps like someone was throwing it off a truck. That was it for the angels.

That's unbelievably kind, she said. You're very lucky.

We are, he said.

You are, she said, to have such a devoted wife.

He blew out a long stream of smoke this time. It spilled against the window as if it were trying to reach out to the snow, its distant cousin.

I think we could be happy now.

I thought so too, she said.

That doesn't seem like a yes, he said.

Her hair was piled up in a bun. He could see the fine delicate line of her jaw when she turned to look out the window. Her dark lashes against her pale skin. The tiny rubies in her earrings that he knew had come from her grandfather's jewelry store. The loose pieces of hair curling at her temple.

This, what's happened, it's forced me to think, she said. I don't think I'm ready for this. She glanced downward.

We don't have to do that yet. There are ways not to. We could start out just the two of us.

I'm not sure I'm even ready for that, she said. She looked up at him. It seemed as though she was going to lean forward and then she didn't. To take you away from her and start something I'm not certain about seems cruel. I can't do that. Not to either of you. I'm not sure anymore I could do it even if I were certain.

The greasy fork sat askew on the pie plate. He picked it up and pointed it at the table.

What happened? What changed?

He looked intently at the fork.

Nothing changed. Everything changed. I still love you.

He laughed a little. He was still looking at the fork. So what will you do?

Now the snow was sticking to the cars and the lampposts. There was a fine dust turning everything silvery and hidden. The sounds of traffic were being muffled. The whistle of the air in the window seemed louder.

She pulled her hand out of her pocket and put something on the table.

I've been taking a lot of long walks lately, she said. I found this for sale and I bought it.

A camera? he said.

A Leica. I've been taking pictures.

That's what you're going to do?

I think so, she said. Do you want to look at it?

He shook his head. She put the camera back in her pocket.

Why can't you do that with me?

Right now I think it's the only thing I want to do.

He felt a slow heavy ache in his solar plexus. His eyes were tearing up. He stubbed out his cigarette in the pie.

What about . . .

I don't know, she said. We have to talk about that.

He was crying.

How could you let it go this far? How could you let me tell Pearl?

I'm sorry, she said. But you also let it go long.

He wiped his face with his sleeve.

That's true, he said.

May I? she said. She reached over and took his coffee cup. He nodded. She held it in her hands. For a moment he had a memory of her bathed in late-afternoon light. Her green eyes. Her hands around a cup. Her indifferent look. He felt it returning. He knew that the feeling in his solar plexus would never go away.

You act like you don't know me, he said.

I love you, Joe, she said. It's me; I don't know. Not yet.

They talked for a long time. Through the fogging window they looked like two blurry figures on film, grainy and flickering and gray. When they stood to leave he took her by the elbow and their silhouettes slid down the long horizontal window of the diner like two shadows walking offscreen.

CHAPTER EIGHTEEN

Milo sat on the bench wearing jeans and a jacket. He still wore the same boots. They were tan leather with dark brown laces and they were stained. He was looking down at them when she walked over to him. She stood right there for a long time and her shadow covered him from the winter sun. She would have been offended that he didn't look up but she realized that he didn't see her. He looked like he could see something in his boots. He looked like he was watching a movie on the ground.

After a while he looked up. His eyes were red. He said: These stories are killing me.

For the first time he asked her to come to his room. It was allowed now. He showed her his single bed. He had a drawing he'd made of her taped up on the wall and some other memorabilia and letters, but mostly the room was plain and nearly empty. They sat down beside each other on the little bed. They were still wearing their coats.

I think I've found you a place to live, she said.

That's great, he said. He was looking down again.

What are you looking at? she said.

My boots, I guess.

What's with the boots?

I told you a long time ago. They belonged to the guy who saved my life.

Why do you wear them?

So I won't forget.

Sometimes it's okay to forget.

Not this time.

All right.

She stood up and took her coat off and laid it on a chair. She sat back down.

This is going to sound strange, he said, but I really don't want to leave this place.

That's not so strange. You've been here a long time. You're used to it. It must feel like home.

He closed his eyes.

Also, I'm thinking, his eyes were still closed and he was clenching his knees, what if it doesn't work when we leave here?

Her hair swung when she leaned toward him. She put her hand on the back of his coat.

There's always that chance, she said. But I'm willing to take it.

I don't mean us, he said. I mean what's happened here, the stories.

I can take that chance too, she said.

But do you want to?

He looked sideways at her. Those yellow flecks in his eyes. Without thinking about it she took her hand off his coat.

Don't you want to know? he said.

She blinked. Her brow was clear and smooth but now it tensed a little and her eyes narrowed.

Yes, she said, looking down, I do. She looked up. But not if it's going to hurt you.

I'm so hurt already, do you think it matters?

Of course it matters. It's enough already.

But you need to know. I can tell. You need this.

I need you more, she said.

I want to do this for you, he said.

Her eyes were tearing now.

When it ends you'll leave here?

When it ends I'll leave.

He had her face in his hands. He kissed her and when he stopped kissing her he took off his coat. Then he reached his hand behind his head and grabbed the back of his shirt and pulled it off. Then he lay down on the bed with his back to her and he took her hand.

The Carriage

The sawdust swirled into tiny piles on the floor when the door opened and closed. A bell rang. The door slammed shut. The wheels of a baby carriage cut smoothly through the sawdust. Behind them, a woman's feet followed in heels and stockings kicking up more yellow explosions of sawdust. The light in the shop was golden and warm. Two men wearing white coats smeared with red worked behind a counter. The woman pushing the baby carriage smiled when she saw them. Hello, Irv, Hello, Arnold, she said. They glanced up from their cutting and shot her friendly looks and said Hello there, ma'am, and How's the baby? There were two women there already and while the woman with the carriage waited she gazed at the pink baby bundled in the carriage and played with her. The infant's face was round and alert and unsmiling although interested in the sudden change of location. Her face registered the dusty air with a quick sneeze. Then it returned instantly to looking up at the lights hanging from the ceiling, the rim of the bonnet of the carriage that caught her vision, the large face of the woman who looked down on her and straightened her cap. The baby kicked off her blanket near her feet and the woman held her feet and said piggies and played with the feet. The infant almost smiled and seemed happy and then looked back at the lights. The woman raised the pitch of her voice and now the baby looked at her, although she did not quite look in her eyes. The woman tucked the feet in their hand-knit booties back underneath the soft blanket.

What's good today, Irv? Did you save me a nice cut?

I have some beautiful lamb chops.

Marvelous. Give me six.

How's the proud papa?

Working hard. He'll be thrilled to have lamb chops.

The man behind the counter wiped his cold wet hands on his apron and began hacking away at some meat. He measured it and wrapped it up in thick white paper and then he tied it up with string. He leaned forward over the counter to hand it to the woman and as he did so he said, Let me see the gorgeous little princess.

The woman turned the carriage around so the man could see.

No, no, lift her up. I need a good look.

The woman removed the infant from her comfortable bedding and lifted her up and showed her to the butcher.

Is she a beauty, the man said.

The woman beamed. The baby squirmed a little. The woman gave her a loving squeeze.

Arnold, c'mere, the man said. Look at her. Look at those gorgeous green eyes.

What was her name?

Who?

The child?

No one said.

I kept searching but I couldn't find out.

Honor had both hands on his rib cage. She moved them around his back. I looked all over. It isn't there.

It's somewhere.

Will you lie on your back? she said.

He shook his head into the pillow.

You can find it without that, he said.

Her hand stopped. She saw a woman rising out from the entrance to a subway station. It was raining slightly when she emerged onto the street.

1973

The rain grew harder. The woman opened an umbrella. It was later, decades later, and although much on the street could have been there when the woman with the baby walked into the butcher shop, you could tell by the clothes, the cars, the style of the streetlights, that time had passed. The woman walked up Lexington Avenue past shoe stores and coffee shops and newsstands that sold cigars. They had black awnings that said Optimo in red. She turned east and headed over toward Second Avenue. She walked down a block of brownstones at the end of which stood a tall brick apartment building and she turned under the awning and walked inside. The doorman said hello.

She got her mail from a wall lined with silver mailboxes. There were letters addressed to Mrs. Alex Michaels. And a postcard that began "Dear Iris." She turned right at the black-and-white sign that read Fallout Shelter and waited for the elevator. She rode up to the twentieth floor. It was one of the last times she would ever enter this building and she was acutely aware of every landmark on her journey home. On her floor she stepped down the hallway and before she had opened the door her little girl was running to her. Mommy, the girl said. The mother scooped up her daughter. She would not tell her that they were leaving yet. Mommy, the girl said, Did you get rained on? Are you wet? Guess what happened!

Tell me everything, Anna, her mother said.

2006

Honor lay down next to Milo in the narrow bed. My mother's name is Anna, she said.

Is she alive? he asked.

Yes, she said.

That's good, he said.

But we haven't seen each other in a long time.

He put his arm over her chest and touched her hair. Why not? he said.

She had me when she was very young, a teenager. It was hard. She wasn't ready for me. Not really ever. I know she loved me but she was not ready and so it seemed as if she was always gone, in the midst of leaving, never really there. I left to become a dancer when I finished high school. I came back to New York where she was from and she didn't want to come back. My grandparents had been very disappointed, and once she left New York they cut her off until she would come back. She didn't. They reached out to her before they died, but she felt it was too late. And by the time I came back they were gone. They both died fairly young.

Where is she now?

I don't even know.

But you could find out.

I suppose so.

Do you think that's her? In the apartment?

Right now I think anything is possible.

She leaned her face on the back of his wide shoulder.

Your body is like a haunted house, she said. And it seems as though I live there.

CHAPTER NINETEEN

Anna

The shadows and reflections chased each other across the ceiling. Cars enacting an endless search party. How did the lights reach up so many stories? She knew she lived on the twentieth floor and it seemed impossible that the tiny automobiles like Matchbox cars so far below could cast such shadows in her room. But what else could it be? Twenty floors, twenty stories, twenty centuries. She should have felt removed from the street and history and the past so high up above but she was always aware of some force coming from behind to catch her. She was only six. She had an Easy-Bake oven and a firing squad of stuffed animals along her bed and she was reading books nearly as big as she was but nothing could protect her from the eternal race on the ceiling of her bedroom, the screaming from the other room.

When they told her they were not going to live together

as a family anymore she thought: Now I understand. The chasing never stops.

So it was with a dark wisdom beyond her years that she had a baby at seventeen. It wasn't done but she did it. (She never told anyone who the father was, and he, with his ski parka and feathered hair and abashed smiles in the cafeteria, never thought to ask or thank her.) If the past was always coming up behind her she thought she might as well turn around and bite it back. She hadn't expected to love the girl so much. She hadn't expected to want to give the girl something so much better. If she had thought it was possible to stop the chasing, she would have done everything differently.

· *2006* ·

I want to know what this has to do with Joe and Vivian, said Honor. What this has to do with us.

It may not have anything to do with us, Milo said. It may just be another story.

But you know it's more than that, she said.

I'm not sure I have as much faith as you do, he said.

It makes no sense if it isn't somehow our story, she said.

Why does it have to make sense? I had to get used to things not making sense.

But you only started to get better when you stopped thinking that way, when you wanted to know what would happen next. When you cared about the stories, about the people, about us.

I still care about you, he said.

Am I enough to keep you going?

He looked at the ceiling. At the walls. No saxophones sliding through them. No scarves billowing down.

For now, he said. I'll keep going until the chasing ends.

They were standing opposite each other, facing each other.

Then I don't want the chasing to end.

She fell asleep. She slept deeply and didn't dream. In the night he rolled over and she woke with her hand on his chest. He was lying on his back.

The sun was a hole in the sky like a cigarette burn. Around it the sky was a pulsing white light that hurt to look at. He looked at it. He had never learned to tell time by the sun but it looked like lunchtime and there wouldn't be any. They were waiting by the side of the road. For something.

The desert stretched out around them and he felt like the first of many figures to be painted on a canvas. Where was everybody else? The artist had up and left. For lunch, he thought to himself and laughed.

What's so funny? the other guy said. His name was Caleb.

Nothing, Milo said.

You laugh a lot, Caleb said.

I guess that's a kind of compliment, Milo said.

To yourself, Caleb said. You laugh a lot to yourself.

Milo looked out at the empty canvas.

It's not because I'm so happy, he said.

Didn't think so, Caleb said.

Why were they just standing there? Milo couldn't

remember. He'd even been told, afterwards, by people who knew, and he could never remember. They had something to do by the side of the road and they were going to be picked up but the truck was late. They were waiting by the side of the road like they were waiting for a city bus.

What's your favorite movie? Caleb said.

That's a hard question, Milo said.

It's not a trick question, Caleb said. Just answer.

Milo scrunched up his face · and looked down and kicked the dusty road.

What's the first thing that comes into your head?

The first thing that comes into my head isn't necessarily my favorite movie.

Caleb turned his face to the side and looked out at the desert. Milo didn't think he was looking for that AWOL artist.

Do you want to know my favorite? Caleb said.

Sure.

I'd have to say it's oh shit there's the truck.

Milo laughed a little. To himself. He saw the truck driving toward them too like a blob of paint at the end of a brush coming nearer and nearer.

They both leaned down to pick up the things they were carrying and had left to rest on the road and small clouds of dust spewed up around their legs and Milo said I guess you'll tell me later and Caleb said sure and then they could both see the truck coming nearer and it didn't look like the kind of truck they were expecting but everything was so fucked up around here that they didn't immediately think anything of it and then as the truck which was coming fast and which looked now to Milo like a whole can of paint being thrown at them from a distance came closer they could see a body lean out the window and it had an arm and the arm was holding something and it was still too far away for them to really see but it was not good and Caleb had been standing to the side of Milo and now for no good reason that Milo could ever think of Caleb jumped on Milo and pushed him down to the ground and Caleb was on top of him so that when the explosion came it came inside of Caleb's person like a body possessed being flung around by an inner demon catapulted by inner fireworks as if the demon were being extinguished and in its place the most beautiful thoughts and brilliant inventions were being visited on the pale and fragile body that remained. Caleb's heavy body lay on Milo for ten hours before Milo heard the other truck. Milo's spinal cord injury made it impossible for him to move and his arms were broken so that he could not push Caleb off. Milo was lying on his back.

CHAPTER TWENTY

When he woke up her arm was no longer on his chest. It was flung above her on the pillow curving around her head as if she were dancing in her sleep. Her face was pointing toward her inner elbow as if there were something written there. He had rolled over and was lying on his front, his face pressed into the pillow. He did not remember or know that he had been lying on his back and that her hand had touched him where the embers burned. He only knew that he was waking with a fear in his ribs and an ache in his solar plexus and a hum of panic in his head. It was as if something terrifying was about to walk through the wall into the room and crush him into the bed.

He felt a sun burning down on him and a weight bearing down on him and then he smelled the smell of flesh and blood hot and sticky against his chest. He pressed his face harder into the pillow. He shut his eyes tight and let out a thin wail but he did not want to wake her she looked so perfect and calm. With each degree of closing his eyes a new image flew toward him: a white sky, a little explosion of dust around a boot and leg, a blob of paint growing closer, a body thrown and jerked in the air by an invisible horse, a head of hair so matted with blood that it looked like a kind of dark sea creature that had attached itself to his chest. Then he saw the whole scene, again, clearly in his mind and he knew that she had found his story.

They say that for some patients the telling and retelling of the story brings relief. For others, it is too much. Milo pressed his face into the pillow for a long time and he wished that he could suffocate the memories. When he thought about them they seemed so banal, just an average wartime disaster, but when he relived them they were his disaster, and that made all the difference. When he thought that Honor now had access to his story he felt ashamed at the paltry nature of his trauma. No massacre, no heroics, no mutiny. Just violence and waiting, mutilation and sorrow, and basic, everyday death. How surprising was that? How special? Was it worth the wait to find out? he wanted to ask her. Did it make him seem even crazier than he was? Wasn't that just what war was?

But then he heard the questions he was asking himself and he realized that he was being cruelest to himself, that of course a dead comrade lying on top of you for hours would leave a trace, a scar, a wound. So if he stopped being cruel to himself about it, what would he do with all that anger? When he had this thought at first he thought: I must be getting better. This is the kind of thing they have been trying to teach me here. How to forgive myself, how to move on. But then a moment later he had a vision of his own death, and he knew that he would never really get better.

Light came in the room from the window. It was night but there were bright lights shining from someplace. She got out of bed, disoriented, and closed the shade. It took her a moment to recognize the little table, the bed, the body sleeping. She had never before fallen asleep here. She wondered why the nurse hadn't woken her and told her visiting hours were over but then she remembered which nurse was on duty and knew that it was one who bent the rules. Honor was wearing her clothes: jeans, socks, a long-sleeved T-shirt. She sat down on the edge of the bed and looked at Milo. He was lying on his front with his face pressed into the pillow. For a moment she was worried that he wasn't breathing. Then she saw the gentle inflation and lift in his rib cage and she could breathe again herself. She talked to him while he slept. She told him that he was going to be okay. She stroked his light brown soft thick hair.

She took off her jeans and slipped back under the covers. Suddenly, he rolled over onto his back. Instinctively, she put her hand on his chest and then she remembered the body inhabited by a demon. He moaned in his sleep. His eyes were still closed. He was clenching his fists and he was crying now. She lifted herself onto him and from up above, for the first time, she touched his face.

1937

The feeling that his life would be a series of revelations, the feeling that Joe had had in the little kitchen while Vivian stood in the weird lavender light that afternoon in September so long ago, was not a feeling he would ever have again. There were no more revelations.

The streets were deserted after dusk.

He walked along the same Brooklyn streets that she had covered so many times without him. He could see her family's house now up the block and he felt his heart pick up the pace and run ahead of him, up the street, up the sloping steps of the dark brownstone. He had put on a tie for this occasion and now he felt too formal and so he took it off and stuffed it into his pocket. He walked faster and then he was standing at the landing. Lights were on within and he waited in the yellow glow. Her mother opened the door. He stepped inside and although he had been to the house only once before he felt oddly at home amidst the heavy carpets and dark wood furniture and he moved down the hall after Vivian's mother as if he had moved down this hall many times before or in a thousand dreams. The older woman floated in front of him like an apparition, paused at the entrance to Vivian's room, and then walked away.

She was sitting up in bed under a faded quilt. She was wearing a demure nightgown he had never seen before. Her hair was down and it fell softly below her shoulders, longer than he had ever seen it. He had not seen her for some time. She put the book she was reading down on the bedside table beneath the lamp with the red silk shade and he stepped forward into the pinkish light.

Come closer, she said.

She nodded her head toward a basket next to the bed.

He looked inside. She's beautiful, he said. She looks like you, he said. He was trying to smile. Vivian reached out her arms and he realized that she wanted him to hand her the baby and with great trembling and a swimming feeling in his head he bent over and picked up the infant and handed her to her mother. Oh Vivian.

And then he broke down. Vivian, he said, are you sure you want to do this?

He would not do this if she had the slightest hesitation. She looked so beautiful, he said, holding her child. And Vivian rocked the child gently and for a moment the girl opened her eyes slowly like nature changing under time-lapse photography and looked up at her mother and then closed them, contented, and fell back to sleep. He kept saying Vivian and he was crying and his hands lay helplessly in his lap and then she said to him:

I'd like to name her Iris.

Of course, he said, whatever you want. A darkness was outlining everything he saw like a border that separated his vision from the rest of the world. Somewhere in the house a door closed. It seemed as though a million doors were closing in his mind each at a slightly different time and the effect was of a virtuosic drumming, a percussion of endings softly building to a final slam.

The baby let out a small cry.

Vivian's face was red and splotchy. She looked like she had been in battle, and she had the worn beauty of the still standing. She looked down at the infant with a weary

expression full of love and unbuttoned her nightgown and
began to nurse her. She seemed older to him, and pos-
sessing a dignity that he knew he would never be able to
approach.

They had been through so much, he said, the two of
them. Was she sure . . .

She did not look at him. She looked at his open collar
and the strength of his neck.

I couldn't do this alone, she said—

You wouldn't have to, he said.

But I don't want to take you away and I need, I need
other things.

She looked at some spot in the air between them. She
seemed fragile and he saw her right eye waver.

I couldn't take care of her the way you can, she said. The
way both of you can.

He could see that she meant it. Her eyes were steady
now, gazing through him.

We will always take care of her, he said.

She shivered when he said this and holding the baby
tightly to her she said Thank you very quietly and with
more tenderness than he had ever seen from her or anyone.

He noticed the way she was touching the child's face
without even thinking about it and he thought she will
never do that again she will never wipe away this girl's
tears or touch the edge of her smile or push her long hair
behind her ear with a finger the way mothers do and he
thought of the girl and would the girl know that she was
missing this even if there was someone else to do those
things and then he pushed the thought away and it was the
last time he could bear to think it.

You must be tired, he said.

I must be but I don't feel it.

Take your time. You tell me when you're ready.

Her hand was touching the tiny perfect hand.

A little longer, she said.

She began to cry.

I don't want to do this, she said. But I have to, you understand?

He nodded.

You can always see her, he said.

She turned her face to the side and shook her head. I don't think so, she said.

The baby slept and together they watched her sleeping. Vivian stared downward with that weary loving look but he could hear the screaming inside her head.

She'll always be yours, he said.

She took a deep breath.

No, she said quietly. But I'll always be hers.

He felt that this was the saddest he could ever be. She was shaking now, holding the baby close and shaking in a kind of rocking motion and the child was sleeping.

He leaned forward and took them both in his arms. For a moment, they were a family. Her wet cheek was pressed against his neck and her arms around the child pushed into his chest and he welcomed the physical pain. He took Vivian's face in his hands and he kissed her for the last time while she cried and shook. I can't do this, she said, looking up at him. And then she handed him the child.

There were fireworks inside Milo, gentle ones like handkerchiefs drooping in surrender and also gigantic and thunderous wheels of light.

Do you have everything? Vivian's mother was standing at the door with Joe while he buttoned his jacket. She handed him a bag filled with blankets and bottles and clothes. She was careful not to look in his eyes. She was holding the door for him now while he reached down and picked up the basket. The yellow light from the house spilled onto the steps and lit his way and then stopped as if giving up against the darkness. He walked into the darkness.

2006

So the baby is Iris, Anna's mother.
    It seems that way.
    And Anna, you think she is . . .
    My mother. I think so.
    Did you know that this is what happened?
    No, I never knew.
    Did you know Pearl?
    No. She died when I was small. And Anna never talked about her.
    Do you want to keep going? he said.
    They were lying side by side. She turned to look at him and he seemed more than tired. His eyes wrinkled at the edges and his lips were pale and dry. The yellow flecks still lit up his blue eyes but the blue was gray now and the flecks seemed like stars hovering at twilight. It was as though his strong physical presence was giving way to something else, making room for something else.

Are you all right? she said.

I'm fine if you are, he said.

I'm not fine, she said. But I want to keep going.

He closed his eyes. He felt her roll back over him, her hair sweeping across his chest and then his face. It was like being in some kind of holy car wash. He thought his body was a vehicle and that she was driving him home, driving him crazy, driving him to the end of the road. He remembered an essay he'd had to read in school and one of the lines in it: Everything good is on the highway. He was a car and she was driving him and they were on the highway and they were lost and they were trying to find everything that was good.

Joe

Joe walked by the river. He never stopped walking by the river. He didn't think that he was looking for anyone, just thinking, and the river helped him think. All the men he knew had to get out of the house sometimes, away from the bills, the lonesome cupboards, the silent cleaning, the baby's cries. He was a father now. He'd take the car and drive downtown even if he didn't have much to do in the office and he'd park and he'd walk past the places he used to go when he was in law school or haunts he'd played in when he was still playing music and he'd always end up heading west toward the river. The river was green today and it reminded him of his daughter's eyes: green and deep and sometimes severe. She was ten now but she could flash her eyes at him like she was a woman, glancing sideways at him flirtatiously one moment, slanted and accusing the next. What was she accusing him of? What did she know? She seemed to know everything, but of course she wouldn't find any of that out until some years later when she came across the original birth certificate hidden among his papers. They had had a false one too, a doctor friend had obliged, but Joe had always kept the original in a file in a drawer in his office just in case, he told himself, just in case . . . he didn't really know why. No, her accusations at this age were more general and, in some ways, more understandable. He was a man filled with guilt and she could smell it and nobody wanted a father weak with guilt. She would have him strong. She would have him able to withstand those green eyes.

But what did he have to feel guilty about? He had made mistakes, everyone makes mistakes, and he did not pretend to be perfect but he had done the best he could given the circumstances. And what were the circumstances? They were the conditions of time and place, America in 1936, where and when he thought his life had ended and begun. A time when the music that he loved played behind everything he felt and did, a music that was considered quintessentially American. But what did that mean? Wasn't it a lie? Because of course, as he had learned, the music only existed, only swung because it was being led by the cymbals and those discs of beaten metal were not American at all but came from someplace far away and long ago. And he remembered the weekend in Massachusetts and the story of Avedis and how the cymbals had come from an Armenian alchemist in seventeenth-century

Turkey, about as far away from Roseland as one could imagine. So the idea that the music had nothing to do with anyplace else, that it was as separate from the world as the country it romanced, this idea was a myth, as all separateness was a fantasy, a dream.

It was the same dream he had fallen into when he met Vivian at the dock, the same fantasy that they could live apart, from the world, from consequences, from Pearl. Like two ships floating in the lenses of a woman's sunglasses. He had been so young. He had been so stupid. He did not regret falling in love with Vivian and he did not regret what they had made of their love. It was a kind of miracle that he was now able to be a father and that their love had resulted in this tender gift for Pearl. But the gift came with so much sadness that he was not always sure that it was worth it. For him, it was worth it. For Pearl, it was worth it. But what about the girl? Joe was not an intellectual and he was not a philosopher but he had become a thinker and the love he had for his daughter led him to thoughts that he would much rather have not had. He no longer experienced the pain he felt that night at Vivian's bedside, he would never let himself feel that again, but his punishment was to be someone who would think and think and think. His mind was a river, and its contents were as green and deep and severe as his daughter's eyes.

He turned up his collar to the wind. He kept walking. His thoughts rushed on, taking him places that he did not want to go. He thought about the future and what his actions would bring in the world. He wanted his daughter's happiness more than anything but he saw that she was not destined primarily for happiness. She was too complicated for happiness. And he wondered what kind of mother she would be, and if he ever lived to see his grand-children what kind of happiness they might know. He felt a pain in his chest. He slowed down. He stopped at a stretch of railing and leaned over and caught his breath. The wind pushed his collar and hair leftward and he had the sensation of leaning over the railing on the deck of an ocean liner many years ago. In the memory he was holding a newspaper and he had folded it into quarters to stop it from flapping in the wind. A notice in the lower right-hand corner of the page caught his eye. It was an advertisement announcing that Count Basie would be making his New York debut on Christmas Eve at the Roseland Ballroom. He remembered reading that and looking out over the sea with anticipation and hope. The ocean that day was navy blue and sparkling with handfuls of diamonds thrown from the sun. The jewels seemed to jump up into the clear air and then alight back on the surface of the water like delicate mystical insects. He thought that this is what life would be: fresh and free and filled with light. But then he thought about returning to law school and he loosened his grip on the paper and the wind stirred up and then the pages flew from his hands. They contorted themselves in various positions of torment as they clutched the railing before breaking free and flying, jerking and buckling and sailing above the water, and then fluttering down to the sea.

That was then, he thought, before Vivian, before Iris, before the war. Everything felt so different now, from the way women wore their clothes with those big shoulders and dramatic hats to the music that people played, swing having long since been left behind by serious musicians. Time swung, he thought, even if the music didn't anymore. He marveled at the way the wind blowing a certain direction could make him feel more than a decade younger and bring him the sensation that he was gazing out at a bright future. The future hadn't turned out too bad, he reasoned. He loved his devoted wife, his beautiful, complicated daughter, his gorgeous suffering cracked and ever-changing city. No, the future wasn't too terrible, he thought. It just didn't really feel like the future anymore.

Iris

The light in the kitchen was dim and silvery blue. Iris was cleaning up the dishes with Pearl when the call came about Joe. He had stayed late at the office. Is your mother home? a voice asked.

She worried that it was something about school. She was fifteen and didn't much like anything but art class although schoolwork came easily to her and she got good grades. Still, her deportment was a problem. She had refused to file her nails for hygiene class. She had said she would prefer to cut them and this defiance had earned her first detention and then a D. She hoped it wasn't that beastly woman calling about some other failure to behave. She liked to wear jeans with the cuffs rolled up. She studied, but she liked the boys who listened to the radio. The teachers noticed things like that. But then she saw Pearl wipe her hands a second time on her apron even though they were dry and tilt her head down and put her hand on the back of the wooden chair and, swaying, move her body into the seat. She pressed the phone to her head as if she were trying to receive a message from a distant planet. Pearl repeated what was being said to her and as she softly mouthed the words Iris's thoughts shattered inside her head. Suddenly the world was trying to reorganize itself and she realized that she would be left with the wrong parent. She loved Pearl but it was for her father that she lived. She felt the truth of this the moment her mother hung up the phone, that there had been a terrible misunderstanding. Your father's had a heart attack, Pearl said, trying to be gentle but sounding to Iris redundant and cold. When her mother left for the morgue Iris refused to go and she did not come out of her room for two days. They had not found Joe until he had already been dead for three hours, and during those two days in her room Iris replayed in her mind everything she had done while he was already gone. She had done her homework. She had listened to the radio. She had eaten dinner with her mother. She tried to tell herself that now everything she did would be like that: she would be doing it while he was no longer alive. If she could go back to not knowing that he was not alive everything might be okay. This was when her fifteen-year-old brain began to blame her mother for having ever picked up the phone. It was several years later that she would find in her father's file cabinets her original birth certificate.

CHAPTER TWENTY-ONE

Honor and Milo

They were driving very fast now. Signs sped past in an imaginary window: Bon Vivant Diner, Used Books, Open Twenty-four Hours. Then they drove straight through the city out onto the road. They were giving themselves over to the highway. Honor had an image of herself and Milo at that moment and they looked to her like a soldier and an angel making love in the backseat of a speeding car. The angel's wings brushed the inside roof of the car and one feathery white tip, gray with soot and exhaust, stuck out the window. The soldier's boots pressed one against the door and the other against the seat and made a rip in the worn vinyl. In this image of herself and Milo, Honor could not tell which one of them was the angel and which one of them was the soldier.

Pearl

Pearl struggled through the blowing sand and occasionally reached for Anna's arm to steady herself. She was absorbed by the task of walking through the desert and could not yet take in her surroundings. Later, when she thought about the last time she had seen her granddaughter and great-grandchild she wished that she had spent more time looking at the girls' faces and less time looking at the sand. The experience of being with Anna in that place again had been overwhelming and unreal and she sometimes wondered if she had actually been there.

The wind had died down and the sand had settled. They reached the top of the dune, where there were two beach chairs waiting for them. Pearl gingerly lowered herself into one of the tiny chairs. She felt a chill although the air was blisteringly hot; she remembered this hot dry weather. The desert stretched out before them but instead of a blank expanse it was strewn with people working and equipment and what looked to her like debris but which in fact was an array of artifacts. A different kind of debris, she thought to herself. She sat atop this mound of sand and was put in mind of generals looking down on a battlefield. Or a director overseeing a film set, she thought, and smiled. She remembered Mr. DeMille and the way he had screeched into his megaphone and stood there silhouetted against the sun like some kind of exotic desert cactus that made noise. If she closed her eyes she could see the Gate of

Ramses II and her small self walking under its enormous archway.

She opened her eyes. There stood the very same archway, in the distance, chipped and broken and slanted but standing up in the desert. And all around were vestiges of *The Ten Commandments:* goblets, chariots, artificial stones. When Anna had told her that her boyfriend was an archaeologist Pearl had imagined the uncovering of ancient tombs and undiscovered hieroglyphs. It seemed like a vaguely noble line of work. But this.

She had been polite about it, and genuinely amazed by the coincidence. Anna hadn't known that her grandmother had worked in film, let alone on the set of this film, and so when she told Pearl that Rob was on a dig in California unearthing an old film set and then said what film it was she had been stunned to hear her grandmother burst out laughing. Pearl was not someone who regularly burst out laughing. It was a short burst. And then Anna had spontaneously suggested that they go out west together to visit the dig. She had never traveled with Pearl and it seemed an unlikely thing to do, but Anna was at that point in her life up for anything, and besides, she had a young child to look after and perhaps Pearl could help. This was unlikely, since Pearl was now in her eighties, but Anna was still, always, expecting everything to turn out in her favor. So she was not really surprised when Pearl agreed to go. Iris thought it was a terrible idea, but this only strengthened both Pearl's and Anna's resolve.

The sun was starting to set and the sky was shimmering with heat. The little girl, Honor, played in the sand. Her hat had fallen off and Pearl thought of mentioning this to

Anna but she was careful not to seem a busybody. It was enough that Anna had remembered a hat, she thought; the girl was still in college. The fact of the child had been absorbed, but nevertheless she worried about Anna's prospects. A single mother. This boyfriend digging for silly props in what was essentially the outskirts of Los Angeles. It was absurd the lengths to which people went to take the movies seriously. She had long ago stopped caring about the movies. She still went, but there was no such thing as glamour to her anymore. Her head was throbbing from the heat, and her vision seemed to be blurring at the edges, but she didn't say anything about it.

Anna asked her questions about her job on the film. What had she done as a wardrobe girl? Was this really where she had met her husband, the grandfather whom Anna had never known? The little girl kept sifting the sand and talking quietly to herself. The sun sank a millimeter lower and the whole sky changed, softening, and the heat lifted a little. Anna stopped asking questions. The workers continued their busy activity in the distance. Pearl settled back into the beach chair. Her head throbbed and the scene before her began to pulse and waver in the heat. She felt faint but she didn't want to trouble Anna. She experienced a dull jolt in the side of her skull like she was bumping her head in a dream and then she knew that she had drifted to someplace unreal. She would stay there, she thought. Just for a moment. Nobody else had to know.

A figure came walking toward them across the sand. It appeared to be a man. Pearl was aware that he had been summoned from her imagination but she did not want to send him back. He was tall and olive-skinned and he was wearing a suit. It was hot for a suit, most of the people working down in the field were wearing T-shirts and jeans, but somehow he did not look strange to Pearl. He approached. As he came closer Pearl tilted her head with curiosity and then stared intently at him.

Do you remember me? he said.

I think I do, Pearl said.

Solomon Eckstein, he said, and held out his hand.

She leaned forward in her little chair and he lifted his other hand and said Don't get up and he knelt down in front of her on one knee and shook her hand. It seemed for a moment like he was going to kiss her hand but he just kept holding it. He held it the whole time they talked.

This is incredible, isn't it, he said.

She thought he was talking about the dig and she said: Who would have imagined that they would have considered this something worth digging up!

No, he said, I meant seeing you again.

Oh, that, she said. She half smiled sweetly and looked off to the side. Well yes, it is incredible.

But it seems right, he said. He looked into her eyes.

Yes, she said, it does.

So, he said, switching his legs and still kneeling, what happened to you? I looked for you when I got out of the infirmary but you were gone.

I went east to start my life, she said, brightly.

How did it go? he said. Your life.

She shifted in her seat and drew her knees in closer. She was aware that her walking sneakers had filled with sand.

It was full, she said. I have a great-granddaughter. She gestured toward Anna and Honor who were burying each other's hands and feet in the sand a little ways away.

That's wonderful, he said.

The sun was setting fully now, sending deep colors, pinks and mauves and oranges and greens, across the sky and the colors seemed to be radiating out from Solomon's head. He looked to Pearl a bit like a religious figure in one of those paintings on black velvet. He was ridiculous and beautiful and she was grateful to him although she couldn't quite remember for what.

I had a family too.

I'm glad.

But I always wondered about you. It's good to see you again.

It's good to see you too, she said.

He held her hand and looked into her eyes for a long time. His eyes were green. Her daughter's eyes were green. That was funny.

He squeezed her hand and stood up and shook the sand from his pants.

Well, he said, I have to go now.

I should be going too, she said. She did not move.

Thank you for everything, he said. And good luck with your family.

You too, she said. Thank you for saying hello.

When Anna came walking back over with Honor, Pearl was wiping her eyes with the back of her hand. Her hand was thin and veined and trembling.

From the speeding car Honor watched herself walk across the desert with Anna and Pearl. Her hat fell off and stayed in the sand as they walked away. She thought: I know now who those people are. She didn't feel anger or sadness or forgiveness or compassion. She just took in the scene and thought: That is the way it was.

She leaned down and kissed Milo and she felt a peace in not having to imagine anymore. Trouble starts, she thought, when we take the symbol for reality. It was a line she must have read in some book Sam had given her. She didn't have to do that anymore, take the symbol for reality.

She saw the three figures walk into the desert and she watched them out the window and she knew for the first time that she had not been letting them go and then the car drove on and she let them go.

That night, in the motel, Honor fell asleep exhausted, still in her clothes, on the second bed. Her face a bright light against the dark maroon bedspread. Her mother marveled at the openness of the child: her mouth wide, her hands upturned, her splayed limbs like disheveled clothes.

Anna was still so young and yet she never slept with her palms open, always curled herself into a ball. If there was one thing she could give her daughter it would be this: to stay open. It would not be an inherited trait, she thought, putting down her toothbrush and turning off the light in the bathroom. Then she crawled into the other bed beside Pearl. It was dark now.

Hi, darling, Pearl said.

Hi, Grandma, she said.

They lay next to each other in the plain room. There was a humming from a generator and lights from the parking lot outside beamed through the drapes and swept across the walls every now and then. They lit up the blank TV screen, the low dresser, the beige wallpaper.

Do you ever regret coming east and leaving the movies? Anna asked.

No, I don't, Pearl said. She was looking straight up with her eyes open. Anna, already falling asleep, couldn't see the tears. If things hadn't happened exactly the way they did, she said, I would never have been here with you.

Milo was also letting go. He could tell that he had given her something and in doing this for her he felt a pressure like the weight of a body, a dead weight, rising from his chest. She looked down on him and she saw the light coming from his face and she felt his ribs nearly burst apart and his arms spread out to receive her and she knew now that it had been she who was the soldier and she saw that he was the angel.

He talked to her in his sleep for the last time. He said they drowned him in the river. He said they came for him in the darkness and they didn't look at him because they knew him.

Who, she said, who are you now?

My name is Parvin, he said.

He said they put a sack over her head and they tied the sack and then they lowered her into a boat. They took another boat and pulled the second boat along behind them and paddled out into the Bosphorous at night. Through a hole in the burlap she could see the stars wobbling on the surface of the water. When they reached far enough they stopped paddling and then they tilted the second boat. When she fell she fell fast and a million bubbles burst around her in an explosion of phosphorescent light.

At the bottom of the river there were hundreds of us, he said, swaying upright like underwater tombstones.

He said this is what they did to the disobedient.

Parvin looked up through the tiny holes in the burlap and saw the shadowy undersides of the two boats slide away on the surface of the water. For a moment, she expected to die there and decided to breathe the water. But then she changed her mind and decided not to die. She had no idea how she would accomplish this, but when she pushed her hands above her head she discovered that the string tying the sack had begun to loosen. She wriggled her hands through the loosening knot and then they emerged through the top of the sack. She wriggled and the sack sunk down to her feet. She appeared to be dancing underwater. Her black hair wafted weightlessly, like ink. It scrawled mad writing behind her as she swam up to the surface for air. She had no time to waste and she swam frantically, but always elegantly, to the far side of the river. There were times when she thought she was too tired to go on, but then she thought of Hyacinth and found strength and continued on.

Still, she could not understand why he had let her be taken away and drowned. He had handed her over to the men who put her in the sack. She had been too confused at the time to feel the full force of this betrayal, but she comforted herself now with the thought that he had done it as part of a ruse, that he had known that the string would disentangle. She could not go on swimming unless she believed this. She could not believe anything else.

What she did not know as she swam was that Hyacinth had given the men the string and that the string had been given to him the night before by Avedis. She did not know until later that during his experiments Avedis had created a rope that looked strong and invincible but which in fact would loosen and dissolve in water. She did not know that Avedis had called for Hyacinth in secret and had given him this string to rescue her from the Sultan. She did not know that Avedis had done this because he loved her and because he knew that she loved Hyacinth.

As she approached the shore she grew weak. The dark water began to lap into her mouth and she could not prevent herself from swallowing it first in sips and then in mouthfuls and then in great and deadly gulps. The land was a dark green mirage that kept slipping up and down, in and out of the water, in and out of her reach. Suddenly she felt that she might die here in the water.

She kept thinking of the last time she had seen Hyacinth, when he handed her over to her murderers. He was standing very still and she could tell now as her head lifted and sunk that he had been frozen with the terror of losing her.

They were driving and it was the dead of night now. In the middle of the night they were speeding across the vast and unknowable country. Then the sky went white and he saw a hole in it like a cigarette burn. He would miss this bed, he thought, it would be hard to leave. He would miss this woman, this night. He would be leaving soon, he knew that now, he could not stay any longer. He was grateful to have had the chance to give her something, but he could not fight for himself. This is what I have been running toward and away from, he thought. This hole in the sky. He could picture himself wriggling through it, ending up on the other side, like some character from a silent comedy or a cartoon strip, always getting into scrapes and miraculously out of them, endlessly emerging from the brink of disaster. But he could not stay here, in this hospital, in this world, any longer. It was impossible. He had used up all of his earthly means of escape.

He looked at the wall with its wide expanse of soft white skin and its subtle shadows changing in the light. He pictured vividly that it would still be here tomorrow, when he was gone. And the pillowcase, he could see the corner of it out of his eye, against the wall, like the collar of a man's shirt against a woman's neck. He could use the pillowcase. He would shred it. Not too thin. It would hold him, as it had held him for so long, only now it would be for the last time. He lay in bed and planned his escape. He said to the wall on which he could project her face into the shadows: Forgive me. I gave you all I could.

What does it mean for a soldier to take his own life after he has survived the war? It depends on the meaning of survival. It depends on the meaning of war. He had nearly given his life for a story about his country, but he didn't believe in that story anymore. Then he had come home and he had kept on fighting and had fought for another story: Honor's. Now he felt that his job was done. To live a life with no story, this was not survival. To begin again, that felt like another war. He had fought. He had lost. He had won. He had loved. He was done. It was over.

·

Parvin did not die. When she finally reached the other side, Hyacinth was waiting for her on the shore. He was holding a bag filled with the coins that Kaya had gathered from the base of the potted plant. He had more of the string that Avedis had invented. "In case of emergency," Hyacinth said. And he had with him a blanket to wrap her up in, he knew she would be shivering and blue, and he carried her to a waiting carriage. Where it was going, Parvin didn't know, and she didn't care.

CHAPTER TWENTY-TWO

Vivian

The photographs were never recovered. Vivian worked with the police and the case remained open for many years, but there were so few clues, so little evidence. And what could possibly have been the motive? The negatives were valuable, but not worth that much, and would have quickly been discovered had they been in circulation. Perhaps there was a mad collector out there who would purchase them, but it seemed unlikely. It appeared that the theft was personal. When the police questioned Vivian about her various relationships and asked her if there was anyone who might wish her harm, she was reminded of all of the mysteries she had ever read and how she had always thought that was a ridiculous question. Of course there must be someone out there who wished her ill, there were any number of random people one slighted in the course of a lifetime, and any number of intimates one would inevitably hurt as well. But she had kept to herself for so long now that unless it was some insanely rivalrous colleague, of which there were too many to count, she could think of no one who would do something like this, and even her fellow photographers were not really capable of stealing. Stealing her ideas, yes, that happened all the time, but her actual pictures? What good would it do? She could always take more.

That's what the director of the museum said to her and that's what she did, over several years. She took hundreds of new pictures, all color now, still of children, still of their moody, mysterious selves and their faces and bodies that continually protected and betrayed them. She finally did have her show, it was not her last, and it was received with great critical acclaim, even helped, perhaps, by the scandal of the stolen photographs. The art world turned out for the opening. It was the early Seventies now. Women's long legs outlined by flowing pants strode across the stone floor of the sculpture garden. Men wore their hair to their shoulders and smiled more than they would a decade later. Older patrons of the museum still dressed in pearls, suits, pumps, handbags, and they mingled with the artists and fashionable younger set like antique ceramic animals mixed in with essential oils and incense on the top of a dresser.

Vivian was surrounded by groups who gathered around her and dispersed. In other words, she was alone. Her hair was slightly shorter these days, still brown, and for the occasion she was wearing a floor-length off-white Indian-style heavy cotton dress with a V-neck bordered with lace. She still looked pretty in a lined but delicate way and much younger than her years, which were approaching sixty. She beamed. She was proud of her work, and gladly accepted compliments. She nodded thoughtfully at people's comments, tilting her head lower the more important the speaker, but listening equally intently, if not more so, when the speaker was a student or a friend. Mostly, though, she was aware of an absence, of her missing pictures, and she winced imperceptibly when she caught sight of a particular image that reminded her of an earlier one that had disappeared. The drinks flowed. People ate Brie on stoned wheat thins. As the night wore on she drank more and felt different feelings, a growing pride as she sensed that the show would mark a major advancement in her career, and a nagging desire, which she thought she had put aside some time ago, to know the truth about the theft. She found herself by the end of the evening desiring to know more than ever who, at the height of her career, had wanted to bring her down.

On the way home from the restaurant where she had celebrated with some museum people and critics and old friends, she caught sight of her reflection in the window of a closed store and stopped. She was wearing a brown coat over her long dress and a scarf tied around her neck. She was struck by something about the coat. It was wool, not too heavy. A spring coat, her mother would have called it, and the way it fell on her, or didn't fall exactly but held its own shape, not accommodating to hers, seemed decidedly old-fashioned in contrast to the flowing dress. It made her look, she thought, like a child. For a second a specific child came to mind, then disappeared in a flash. The image of the child reminded her of earlier lives she had led and the coat reminded her of the shapes she had tried to fit into throughout her life. She felt the childishness of her own inability to either adapt to the shape or throw off the coat.

She would never, she realized, have been happy adapting to the cut of the coat. She should have learned that by now, but still there were times when she felt haunted by an uneasy feeling that she was not living the correct life, that she should never have become an artist. But it was too late. And anyway now she understood: Every choice would have brought some kind of pain. This life was the correct life. This was who she was.

She walked to the corner and waited for the light to change. There was a metal garbage can on the sidewalk, debris moving around inside it as the late April wind blew a little stronger than gently and the blue-gray underwater light of the city streets in the early morning appeared to make objects float. The traffic light seemed to take forever. She stared up at the yellow fixture suspended above the street, and within it the illuminated red circle. A bright orb pulsing against the dull colors of the faded night sky, the looming neutral buildings. Another memory formed and then disintegrated in her mind. She felt a shift inside as if she had remembered a name that she had been trying to summon all day, or for decades. She couldn't have said what the name was, but she knew that something she had worried about was no longer worth troubling over. She knew that her stolen pictures were safe. The light changed again while she thought this and instead of crossing the street right away she stood there and took off her coat.

The breeze felt good. She let the cool unclean air ripple through her long dress. She cradled the coat in her arms for a while. Then she folded the coat and settled it into the garbage can, nestled among the newspapers and wrappers and food. The light changed. She crossed the street. She left the coat. She headed home.

Iris

After Iris and Alex got divorced, Iris moved with Anna to the West Side. They lived in a rent-stabilized apartment in the Nineties on West End Avenue where the rooms branched off of a long narrow hallway like pages falling off the spine of an old book. Guests were always getting lost and ending up in the pantry by way of the maid's bathroom. Of course there was no maid. Alex remarried and lived on Park Avenue and Anna spent her weekends with him and his new family. Sunday nights she would return home to Iris, watch some *Masterpiece Theatre* with her mother, and fall asleep to the sound of Iris's typing, the quick footsteps of little intellectual mice. Iris had become a journalist. When friends asked Anna what her mother wrote about she would say: Pretty much anything. And that was true. She had written everything from restaurant reviews to celebrity interviews to investigative pieces about insurance fraud or water safety. Eventually, Iris remarried as well, but it didn't last long, and when it was over she decided that marriage was not for her. Shortly after, Anna gave birth to Honor, to Iris's horror and chagrin, and it was really only then that Iris discovered the meaning of familial pleasure. Honor she adored. The child returned her affection, not caring if Iris showed up two hours late for a visit or if she spent the whole time talking about her latest article. Iris oozed love for the little girl and would look at her with a gaze of such acceptance and devotion that the child could not help but fall into her grandmother's arms. This was helpful, since her mother was still in school.

One day Honor was at her grandmother's house while Anna studied in the library for her graduate school entrance exam. The little girl wandered freely around the apartment. Iris was at her typewriter. It was 1988. Outside, the world was gleefully throwing off the old habits of book learning and face-to-face communication in favor of newer, more technologically advanced and faster methods of progressing in life without having to actually experience it, but in Iris's apartment the walls were lined with the soon-to-be-relics of print culture, although they did not know yet of their imminent irrelevance and so stood proudly at attention or jauntily slanted and at ease at their posts. Honor loved to pull out a bunch of them and use them to build castles as if they were blocks, but now she was getting old enough to enjoy flipping through them and studying the pictures or the tiny letters which she was just beginning to understand could interact with one another to make sense.

The narrow hall was a dim haze. The dust motes blanketing the bookshelves that lined the passage swirled frantically when Honor passed, like thousands of tiny fish disturbed by a great ship. The little girl, not yet five, knelt down to scan the lowest shelves and found a gigantic book, *The History of Italian Art,* lying on its side. It was a huge linen-covered tome missing its glossy wrapping and when Honor opened to the middle the smooth pages buckled and swelled in a wave and out rolled a faded piece of paper the size and shape of a ticket stub. It wafted to the ground, and was blown, who knows by what wind, through the space under a door that Honor had never before noticed.

It was a thin door, inconspicuously located at a break between the shelves, painted a graying white just like the shelves and walls, and it had a fancy cut-glass doorknob. Honor instinctively lifted herself up onto her tiptoes and turned the knob. Here was a closet, stuffed with shopping bags that in turn overflowed with more stuff. The door had obviously been squeezed shut against the tide of unwanted things that could not be parted with, and so with its opening a few bags were dislodged and one spilled its entire contents onto the floor.

It was a bag of photographs. Contact sheets, individual prints, little plastic boxes of slides, vellum packets of shiny negatives, they all tumbled out at Honor's feet. She looked down at them as if jewels from a treasure chest had spilled in front of her. She sat down. She made herself comfortable among the heap of things obviously so unnecessary that they had been hidden away and not missed. She felt at liberty to play with them. There was no one and nothing to stop her. She noticed a pen idling on the floor of the closet, toward the back. She crawled over the photographs and stretched her arm into the closet and grabbed the pen. It was a blue ballpoint. The top had been chewed. She pulled it off, picked up a large contact sheet covered with black and white images of children, and began to write her name, or her approximation of it, over the images. Then she drew heart shapes and flowers and designs that looked like stars. She drew suns with rays of different lengths angling out in every direction. She made circles and spirals and what she thought looked like staircases. She made a garden. She drew a mother and child.

She went through her entire repertoire of favorite subjects and worked her way over the contact sheets, the individual prints, then onto the tiny slides, their stiff white edges bordering miniature worlds of transparent colors, and then, finally, to the negatives, on which the blue ballpoint pen hardly showed up at all, other than to obscure the darkened faces and whitened backgrounds which already seemed dementedly drawn by some wild child. She took exquisite pleasure in her project. She worked with concentration and deep thought and she was fortunate that her grandmother, who eventually realized that she had not heard from her normally talkative granddaughter in over an hour, found the sight of Honor scribbling across the contraband photographs which she had absconded with so many years ago shocking but not enraging, disturbing but not worthy of raising her voice. She had changed. She was not the person who had stolen the photographs, not anymore. She would always be angry and difficult and filled with a sense that she had been robbed of the right parent, but she didn't pay quite so much attention to those feelings after so many years. And she could forgive anything Honor did. That was love. If this was what it took to enable her to experience some love, then it was worth it. Everything, in this moment, seemed worth it.

That evening after Anna had picked up Honor and taken her home, Iris cleaned up the mess in the hallway. She took a garbage bag from the kitchen, the old Bergdorf's bag was torn and had ripped nearly in half when it fell, and began picking up the pictures and putting them in the plastic bag. For the first time, she tried to really look at them, but now they were covered with the shiny lines and scrawls and indentations of the ballpoint pen. Here and there she could make out a face or a hand, sometimes the sense of a whole composition, and she had the distance now to see the photographs for what they were: works of art. She still felt personally enough about them to find it amusing and strangely satisfying that they had been defaced by her granddaughter, but she also recognized the loss that this represented. She had followed Vivian's career and knew that the images would be worth a fortune, although she had long ago given up the thought of having a fortune of her own and had never really contemplated trying to sell them. No, however unethically, she still considered them her birthright, and now, at the age of fifty-one, she had mellowed to the point of feeling like this was the perfect use and manifestation of her inheritance.

She picked up the last picture. Underneath it, lying on the floor, was a yellowed piece of paper, the size and shape of a ticket stub. It was a ticket stub. The writing on it was faded but she could just make out that it was for a performance of Count Basie's Orchestra at the Roseland Ballroom on Christmas Eve 1936. She threw it in the bag. The last thing she picked up was the book on Italian art. It had been among her father's possessions. She didn't notice as she closed it that it was inscribed to Joe and Pearl, from V. "One day I hope you get to see these pictures," it read.

Anna

After her daughter moved to New York City and made it clear that she wanted the space and freedom to make her own life, far from the confusing influence of a somewhat unbalanced mother, Anna had found work at a small college in the Midwest and had made some effort to stay in touch with Honor but had not pushed it. After all, she had hardly been in close touch with her own mother in later years, and now that Iris was gone she guiltily enjoyed the feeling of unfettered—some would say unmoored—freedom from having no attachments to any generation but her own. Her daughter, she often thought, was probably better off without her. Anna drifted from job to job, relationship to relationship. It didn't feel like drifting to her. Each entanglement felt heavy with meaning and purpose, every new employer held forth the promise of complete security and comfort. Eventually, however, the constant inconstancy caught up with her, and she accepted an administrative position at a junior college on Long Island, where she could have a nice apartment in a small house a short distance from a beach. She supplemented her income by giving music lessons. Her one indulgence was an upright piano. She still loved music. Sometimes she took down the old saxophone from the back of a closet and played a little, although she had never been any good.

When the days grew longer she would walk along the beach after dinner. She scanned the shore as if she were expecting a bottle to wash up, addressed to her. She still wrote to Honor, on holidays and her birthday. She mailed the letters to whatever address she had. Occasionally her daughter sent a postcard, but she had not received one in a long time.

The sky was white and the sea was almost black. Hundreds of triangles of light floated on the surface of the water, silver and shifting, making the ocean look as if it had been sketched in pencil. A boat or two sailed away. Anna looked around and wondered how she had ended up here. She had been raised in privilege, attended an elite high school, been derailed by a teenage pregnancy, but still, out here in what felt like nowhere, how did that happen? She felt the nowhereness of her place on the planet and smiled. She asked herself why she hadn't asked herself the more important questions: How was it that she had ended up here and could still feel so happy? How was it that the light on the water could soften the piercing sense that her life had sailed away? Was this a gift she possessed, this ability to inhabit the present so completely and contentedly, or was it a curse? The tendency that had turned at various times in her life to distractedness or impulsiveness or, to put it mildly, low frustration tolerance and poor planning. Who knew? She had always felt as though she was waiting for something and she had cultivated a kind of perverse patience, a patience that rarely seemed like wisdom but which—from a great, great distance, the kind she had now, here, looking at the vast expanse of liquid spilling off the side of the earth—now seemed to her the essence of her being. She had had the patience to have her daughter young and wait for her own youth to happen later. She had had the patience to let her daughter go and know that time would bring what it would bring. Maybe these were rationalizations. It didn't matter. This is the way things looked to her now.

The sky was still white. The sea was still black. The other wanderers on the beach were still wandering. A figure came walking toward her across the sand. It was a man. He was slightly younger than Anna, weathered for his age, sandy-haired. He was barefoot. He knew her. He smiled when he approached and he wrapped his arms around her. Perhaps he was why she felt happy now.

They walked together along the water. They talked of their short-term plans: dinner, a boat ride this weekend, maybe they would get a dog. Then they fell silent and continued to walk. Anna thought about the loneliness she felt in spite of her contentment, a loneliness that echoed through the generations, and how it was so much a part of her by this age that she didn't notice it sometimes. So maybe she should have called it a contentment in spite of her loneliness. But what was the initial sound that was still echoing? Where did this come from? She would never know, but she hoped that someday perhaps her daughter would. Her daughter. She kept coming up today, or maybe it was every day and Anna was only just noticing it. The light had shifted and the water was shimmering dully like an enormous stretch of tinfoil, and the sky had gone from white to the kind of pale blue that emerges just before sunset begins, a last gasp of day. Her daughter. She would be twenty-one.

Anna stopped walking. She bent over. Her companion asked her if she was okay. He bent down too. They stayed that way for some time and just as he began to get really worried and ask if he should call a doctor she shook her head and said I'm fine and stood up.

Actually, she said, I'm not fine. But that's okay.

Her daughter. To say she missed her did not capture the stormy magnitude of her wanting. She could feel the full force of it now. What had happened? Just a shift of light on the water? Maybe that was all it took to realize that this life of contentment in the present was only possible by forgetting the past. And something, some shade of blue or gray or brush of wind or smell of salt, had brought back a hint of the past or perhaps a whiff of the future and suddenly the disconnectedness required to live in only the present, a present that one could convince oneself was luminous with the Now but which in fact was cut off like a sound dampened in mid-beat, this disconnectedness no longer satisfied. No, it was not possible to really be in the present without feeling the hard-won losses of the past, the clear terror that was the future. To ignore where all of these feelings came from, where it all began, that would be like thinking a song came from nowhere, a romance from nothing, a country sprung fully formed from itself. Trouble started this way. How to end it? Anna had no idea. All she had was a sense that by allowing the longing in, the excruciating desire, she might see more fully and maybe have access to some ragged shred of wisdom. Maybe. And maybe they would get a dog.

CHAPTER TWENTY-THREE

The forsythia bloomed and there were low fireworks of bright yellow all around the park. Then the dogwood bloomed and the magnolia trees bloomed and then the cherry blossoms and pear blossoms came next and the flowering trees canopied the entire park and underneath the trees the shade was cool and the light filtered down between the leaves in shapes that resembled a second blanketing of shadowy flowers tossed all over the green grass. People brought picnic baskets and arranged themselves in groups on the lawns as if they were posing for a grand picture and in the pond there were turtles and the children ran up to the pond and stopped and threw pieces of bread to the turtles and an egret swooped down from on high every once in a while and gave the onlookers a start and something to gaze at in amazement. By the pond one little girl stood with her back to the water watching the people as they watched the egret. She was wearing a princess-style wool coat in red with gold buttons and she was hot but her mother had made her wear it. It was a spring coat, her mother had insisted, and it was chilly out, but the child knew she was wearing it more for show than for comfort. They had cousins in the children's clothing business who had given her the coat and who would be meeting them later that day. The girl ignored her coat. She watched the adults. She watched them so intently with her serious little eyes that it was almost as if she were looking for something, or someone. Her vision landed on pocketbooks and high-heeled shoes and children in sailor suits that were old-fashioned even for the time. Those children were worse off than she was! Then finally out of boredom she looked at the pond.

A woman came walking up the path toward the pond. She noticed the girl in the red wool coat. She glanced around to see where the girl's mother or father might be and she didn't see anyone right nearby who fit the description. Then she saw a little ways off a couple that she had to look away from as soon as she saw them. They were sitting under a nearby tree eating sandwiches from a picnic basket and they were not concerned about their daughter, as they had no need to be. They were in Central Park. It was 1943. She was perfectly safe.

The woman stood next to the little girl. The little girl looked down just past her feet at the edge of the water where the turtles swam and hovered and waited for food.

I don't have anything for you, the girl said to the turtles.

I might have something, the woman said. Would you like me to check?

The little girl twisted her head to the side and tilted it up and looked at the woman for the first time and said yes without smiling or saying please or thank you. The woman didn't mind.

She opened her pocketbook and found some crackers wrapped in a napkin.

Here, why don't you take these.

All right.

The girl broke off some bits of the crackers and tossed them down to the water where the turtles glided toward them and snapped them up.

They were hungry, the woman said.

They're always hungry, the little girl said.

Do you come here often? the woman asked.

On weekends, the girl said. She looked up again at the woman. Her hair was soft and dark and brown. She was wearing pretty earrings with little rubies in them.

Once when I came here a man told me you're not supposed to feed the turtles because it's bad for them and could make them die. I wouldn't want to hurt them but they do look hungry so I almost always end up feeding them.

Then she told the woman about her school, how she liked to paint, about her parents, how they always made the same kind of sandwiches every weekend. But they were good.

She asked if the woman had any more crackers. The woman glanced off to the side and saw that the girl's parents were occupied and said let me see and knelt down and said let's check in my pocketbook.

When the woman opened her pocketbook again the little girl saw something inside that interested her. What's that? she said, pointing to it. A camera, the woman said. Oh, the little girl said. Do you have any more crackers?

The woman didn't and the girl looked disappointed. But then she recovered and said, Sometimes an egret comes. He was here before, but then he flew away.

He'll come back, said the woman.

I know, said the little girl.

The two of them stood together looking out at the water.

You're a very smart and interesting little girl, said the woman.

The girl's face brightened. People usually only told her that she was pretty or good.

Thank you, she said. Then she smiled at the woman.

The woman was about to say something else when the little girl said, Oh that's my mother waving to me. I have to go now.

Good-bye, said the girl.

Good-bye, said the woman. The woman waited awhile for the egret to come back. She waited a long time, and it never did.

CHAPTER TWENTY-FOUR

When Honor showed up on Anna's doorstep she was carrying her infant son in a sling. Anna opened the door and on her face was a look of suffering and longing and welcome.

I see you've brought someone with you, she said.

History repeats itself, said Honor.

If you don't watch out, said Anna.

They ate dinner in silence, except for the noises made by the baby, the sudden gulps of air and exhalations of pleasure that accompany the beginning of life. In the quiet Honor felt stirrings of the beginning of her own life and Anna did too. A feeling that in stillness they could find more than momentary relief, more than a sudden abatement of despair. Here was a chance for something other than happiness. Something like harmony.

She had said good-bye to Milo thinking that she would see him the next day, that they would continue planning their new life. She realized in retrospect that this had been her fantasy. He had not really given her much reason to believe. But she had believed anyway. She had come to the hospital the next day—the nurses had not been able to reach her—and that was when she had seen his room, which was already empty of him. She opened the door and a pure whiteness filled the space completely and she looked for him in the shadows but there were no shadows. Someone came up behind her and quickly closed the door.

On the way home and for a long time she would see him and hear him and speak to him. They had so many unfinished conversations. She saw his face, heard his voice, felt his skin, and sometimes she relived their times together.

He is lying face down on the table with a sheet over him, in a posture of near death, but his body so alive. His arms are beside him, his fists are clenched, his eyes firmly closed. One of the muscles in his back twitches as she touches him. His fist tightens. She is frightened and thinks: How can he have so much pain? What is he feeling? And then he begins to speak.

We died that night at Roseland, he says. And as he talks he pulls her into the story. But in this memory they enter the story entirely and together. Just as she wishes it could have been. In this memory they are inside a memory, side by side in a slowly moving car. It is night and they step onto the sidewalk. The world glitters. She squeezes his hand. They dance together. She is sitting on the subway and at the same time somewhere else they are dancing, the two of them, together.

Honor slept on a pull-out couch in the living room, the baby curled beside her. That night she had strange and radiant dreams and when she woke up she had a visitor.

So many visions, he said, so few visitors.

Hello there, she said to the darkness.

Her eyes adjusted. It was blue in the room. There were no shades. The night poured in.

I couldn't go on, he said.

I know, she said.

I'm sorry, he said.

I miss you.

They were quiet in the darkness for a long time.

Your son is beautiful, she said. Look.

I'll always be looking, he said.

Outside, cars and voices and life went on in the distance. Then silence. Then she understood that her soldier was gone.

She sat up in bed and held the baby.

Tell our son where he comes from, the voice in her head spoke.

I will.

Tell him our stories.

I will.

Once upon a time there was a place where the music always played. American music blew like smoke out the windows. A dance palace where the people spun around and around, circling endlessly in the swing of time. Men lifted their legs and the sharp creases in their pants broke and their cuffs batted their socks and their leather shoes shone. Women threw their heads back and their hair flew out behind them like water flung from a glass. Everything seemed original and free. The voices of the instruments called out innocent and strong. The piano keys pushed the hammers and the hammers hit the strings and the strings pulled the hearts of a country. The songs were simple and the words were sometimes beautiful and sometimes they broke your heart. And the people sang them anyway.

ACKNOWLEDGMENTS

The author wishes to thank: Ann Close, for her loyalty and wisdom. Melanie Jackson, for her intelligence and guidance. Caroline Zancan and everyone at Knopf, for all their expertise. Melissa Marks, Pamela Kottler, Alice Naude, Andrew Solomon, Rachel Abramowitz, and Cynthia Zarin, for friendship and reading. Stephen Bitterolf, for assistance a long, long time ago. Deborah Joy Corey and Bill Zildjian, for telling me that there was a secret formula for making cymbals. My parents and the extended Mendelsohn and Davis families, for their love and support. My husband, Nick, for every day. And, finally, my daughters, Lily Johanna and Grace Isabel—everything you do and say is music to me.

ALSO BY JANE MENDELSOHN

I WAS AMELIA EARHART

In this brilliantly imagined novel, Amelia Earhart tells us what happened after she and her navigator, Fred Noonan, disappeared off the coast of New Guinea one glorious, windy day in 1937. And she tells us about herself. There is her love affair with flying. There are her memories of the past: her childhood desire to become a heroine ("Heroines did what they wanted"); her marriage to G. P. Putnam, who promoted her to fame, but was willing to gamble her life so that the book she was writing about her round-the-world flight would sell out before Christmas. There is the flight itself—day after magnificent or perilous or exhilarating or terrifying day. There is, miraculously, an island. And, most important, there is Noonan.

Historical Fiction

VINTAGE BOOKS
Available wherever books are sold.
www.randomhouse.com

Meet with Interesting People
Enjoy Stimulating Conversation
Discover Wonderful Books

VINTAGE BOOKS / ANCHOR BOOKS ⚓

Reading Group Center

THE READING GROUP SOURCE FOR BOOK LOVERS

Visit ReadingGroupCenter.com where you'll find great reading choices—award winners, bestsellers, beloved classics, and many more—and extensive resources for reading groups such as:

Author Chats

Exciting contests offer reading groups the chance to win one-on-one phone conversations with Vintage and Anchor Books authors.

Extensive Discussion Guides

Guides for over 450 titles as well as non–title specific discussion questions by category for fiction, nonfiction, memoir, poetry, and mystery.

Personal Advice and Ideas

Reading groups nationwide share ideas, suggestions, helpful tips, and anecdotal information. Participate in the discussion and share your group's experiences.

Behind the Book Features

Specially designed pages which can include photographs, videos, original essays, notes from the author and editor, and book-related information.

Reading Planner

Plan ahead by browsing upcoming titles, finding author event schedules, and more.

Special for Spanish-language reading groups

www.grupodelectura.com

A dedicated Spanish-language content area complete with recommended titles from Vintage Español.

A selection of some favorite reading group titles from our list

Atonement by Ian McEwan
Balzac and the Little Chinese Seamstress by Dai Sijie
The Blind Assassin by Margaret Atwood
The Devil in the White City by Erik Larson
Empire Falls by Richard Russo
The English Patient by Michael Ondaatje
A Heartbreaking Work of Staggering Genius by Dave Eggers
The House of Sand and Fog by Andre Dubus III
A Lesson Before Dying by Ernest J. Gaines

Lolita by Vladimir Nabokov
Memoirs of a Geisha by Arthur Golden
Midnight in the Garden of Good and Evil by John Berendt
Midwives by Chris Bohjalian
Push by Sapphire
The Reader by Bernhard Schlink
Snow by Orhan Pamuk
An Unquiet Mind by Kay Redfield Jamison
Waiting by Ha Jin
A Year in Provence by Peter Mayle